"I want to ... Cassie— ... "

Paul's hands were clamped on her shoulders and he drew her to him so that her cheek pressed against the rough fabric of his coat.

"It's *I* who have to forgive *you*," she told him dully. "Though I don't think I ever can."

"Why must you persist..." He shoved her rudely away from him. "Why can't you tell me the truth even now?"

"I thought you loved me, but instead you believed all those lies about me." Cassie's voice was shaking and she took in a deep breath. "It was not me, Paul. I did not telephone your contact. And I never breathed a word of it to Keith. He didn't get the tip-off from me."

"I *want* that to be the truth," he said slowly. "More than anything."

PIPPA CLARKE was born and raised in South London, where she works as a journalist and commissioning editor at the *Sunday Times Magazine*. She has also done two stints as an "agony aunt," writing advice columns under a pseudonym for various magazines. Although she is a relative newcomer to romance fiction, the author has written numerous short stories and has had two novels published.

Books by Pippa Clarke

HARLEQUIN PRESENTS
944—THE PUPPET MASTER

Don't miss any of our special offers. Write to us at the following address for information on our newest releases.

Harlequin Reader Service
901 Fuhrmann Blvd., P.O. Box 1397, Buffalo, NY 14240
Canadian address: P.O. Box 603,
Fort Erie, Ont. L2A 5X3

PIPPA CLARKE

dancing in the dark

Harlequin Books

TORONTO • NEW YORK • LONDON
AMSTERDAM • PARIS • SYDNEY • HAMBURG
STOCKHOLM • ATHENS • TOKYO • MILAN

Harlequin Presents first edition September 1987
ISBN 0-373-11009-X

Original hardcover edition published in 1986
by Mills & Boon Limited

CHAPTER ONE

LORRAINE had done the impossible—she had emasculated the room. 'What do you think?' she asked proudly, teetering on the desk-top in stiletto heels and admiring her morning's handiwork.

Festoons were looped from the four corners of the ceiling to the light-fittings, silver foil stars twirled on invisible threads, while spray-on snow blanked out some of the precious daylight which tried to find its way in through the grimy window-panes from the central well where the ducts and fans complained noisily all day about having to supply warmed, filtered air to the building.

'It looks . . .' With some reluctance, Cassie Murray pushed her typewriter away from her and sat back to survey the result of her secretary's efforts. 'Very festive,' she pronounced with a smile. 'And,' she thought ruefully, 'very feminine.'

The offices of the *Sunday Monitor* had always seemed to her uncompromisingly male—dingy, spartan and colourless. It was not an atmosphere in which she would ideally have chosen to work. All the same, though she would not for the world have offended Lorraine by telling her so, she was none too sure about the bower she had created. As editor of the women's pages, the *In Touch* section and, at twenty-six, one of the youngest section editors on Fleet Street, Cassie knew all about chauvinism. Newspapers were a man's world. Perhaps ninety per cent of her colleagues were men. What would they make of the fancy bits and frippery which now adorned her place of work? And how might the image of cool professionalism which she was ever trying to promote, be undermined by so much tinsel?

5

'I'm glad you're pleased.' Lorraine, never very alive to nuances of expression, glowed with pleasure. 'It looks so much more Christmassy now, doesn't it?'

'It does that.'

'And more homey.'

'Certainly more homey.'

'I bought the decorations in Leather Lane market. All this lot . . .' Lorraine indicated the festoons with an airy wave of the hand, 'for three quid. I raided the kitty. We'll have to collect some more coffee money this afternoon.'

'All right.'

'D'you think we've got enough?'

'What, coffee?'

'No, decorations. I could get some more when I go for lunch.'

Lunch? Did that mean that there was a chance—a faint glimmer of hope—that Lorraine could be persuaded to go out and allow Cassie half an hour of peace and quiet in which to finish writing her copy? 'You could take your break now, if you liked,' she proposed.

'And you think this is enough? Only they've got these little paper snowmen and Father Christmases——'

'I think it's fine as it is. We don't want to overdo it.'

Oxford Street, Regent Street, Las Vegas by night, the Blackpool illuminations . . . all paled in Cassie's imagination beside the garnish and gaudery which now surrounded her. She drew her typewriter back towards her and rattled away at the keys—a hint.

'You don't want me to sort out the letters for *Keep In Touch* before I go?'

'No, it's all right, Bridie's seen to it.' Bridie McKay, Cassie's stalwart sub-editor, had that morning gone through the correspondence for their weekly talk-back column, had chosen the readers' letters to be published, edited them with her incisive pen, and sent them down to the printers. The galley proofs would be up any minute.

'My, my, isn't this jolly?' At that moment, John

Stirling, Labour Correspondent, breezed in. He cast a cursory eye over the decorations before turning his attentions to Lorraine where she stood on the desk—to the distractions of a short leather skirt and long, shapely, black-stockinged legs.

'Did you want something, John?' Cassie asked him pointedly. He was a nice enough man, in his forties, married with children, but, like so many of them, behaved as though he were Jack the Lad.

'I was just wondering . . .'

Innocent, Lorraine flashed a lean thigh as she eased herself off the desk on to the floor; Cassie had to wait a moment to learn just what it was that the preoccupied John had to say.

'I'll be off now.'

'All right Lorraine.'

'I just wondered . . .' John followed the young secretary's movements as she slipped into her coat and made for the door. 'I thought you might fancy a tincture, Cass.'

'A drink? I don't know. I have my column to finish. I haven't been able to get on with it for all the interruptions.'

'Take a break,' he counselled, blithely ignoring the jibe. 'Come to it fresh. That's what I do when I have a mental block.'

'I don't *have* a block.' Cassie sighed. 'I just need a bit of peace and a chance to concentrate.'

'Well, when you're through I'll be over the road. Wine bar. Join me.'

'I'll have to see, John. I don't know, I might.'

'Do you good. All work and no play and all that. Oh, by the way . . .' He was about to leave, and turned to impart the news with an assumed casualness designed for maximum impact. 'Heard the latest? Nick Moy's resigned. Had a row with the Mighty Atom and walked out. *Prud'homme*'s up for grabs. No prizes for guessing who'll land the job, mind. Roth's been recalled from New York and he's always been a hot contender.'

When John had gone, Cassie pondered this latest snippet of office tattle. Anthony Holt, the Editor, alias Ant, Atom Ant and The Atom, was a gifted and able man, small and dynamic, with a ruthless streak and an unwavering belief in his own rightness. So Nick Moy had chosen to cross swords with him and had been the loser! It was a shame. She had liked Nick and he had been excellent as *Prud'homme*, which was the soubriquet of the paper's gossip columnist. It was one of the most coveted positions among journalists. Traditionally a male preserve, it called for a dogged newshound, a super sleuth, and someone of taste, intellect and discrimination, the sort of man who would feel equally at ease in the company of top politicians, film stars and royalty, if he were not to turn the job into a scandal-mongering exercise unworthy of a quality paper like the *Monitor*.

By all accounts, Paul Roth would fit the bill admirably. In her six months on the paper Cassie had not met the New York correspondent, but she had admired his writing, his stylish prose, sardonic humour and no-nonsense attitude that seemed very much at one with the handsome, half-smiling face which appeared above the longer of his contributions. Despite a certain sadness for Nick, she couldn't help relishing this unexpected development. The winds of change were always bracing.

But ... work to be done, she reminded herself, and she bent over her typewriter to daub with correcting fluid at one ill-chosen phrase, succeeding only in making an ugly white splurge.

Maybe John had been right, she should take a short break. Besides, curiosity to hear the news in more detail was beginning to get in the way of creative flow. She picked up her bag and nipped along to the ladies' loo to comb her hair and repair her make-up before going out.

Cassie Murray, journalist, stared solemnly out at her from the tarnished and slightly distorting mirror. Cassie Murray, editor, award-winning young writer. This was

the persona she preferred, the one she lived and
breathed.

She did not see—did not recognise—the beauty in
that elfin face, the delicate high cheekbones, the wide
brown eyes. Her hair was dark; she pushed it tidily
behind her ears. She was slight of build with the pretty,
youthful figure of a schoolgirl, yet her clothes—no-
nonsense blouse and grey wool slacks—were a denial of
all her feminine attributes. She was not much concerned
with looking attractive. More than that: she was much
concerned with *not* looking attractive. Presentable, yes;
sexual, no.

It would have been easy enough to enjoy a flirtatious
relationship with her colleagues, to be flattered by their
attentions, to fall into the gender trap. But then, who
would take her seriously? She well understood how her
looks might draw the eye away from her other—and, to
her, more important—distinctions. Little chance, then,
of landing another job, a promotion to a weightier
section. The women's pages, for all that she had
brought to them an abrasive feminism, for all that they
were aimed at the thinking reader, were still considered
essentially frivolous. And unless the senior editorial
staff could be persuaded to take *her* in earnest, what
chance was there of winning respect for what she *did*?

That was how she had rationalised her attitude,
explained it to herself. The reason she played down her
appearance. A heartbreak at university, an episode of
tears, had nothing whatever to do with it. Oh,
goodness, no!

And it was a source of grim satisfaction to her that
she was known at work variously as blue-stocking and
ice-maiden, for she knew this to be mere stereotyping
by those who felt their masculinity threatened. She did
not fancy them, the male illogic went, so she must be
either a stuffy academic or plain frigid. It was really
rather amusing. It would make a horse laugh.

Decisively she clamped her hair back with a slide.
Now for that drink.

In the down-going lift she met one of the bearded, long-cardigan brigade from the Literary Department.

'Hello, Aubrey,' she said warily.

'Hello, Cassie.' He bared yellowed teeth like piano keys in a lascivious leer. He stood that bit too close. The blue-stocking image, she realised, was not a turn-off to quite everyone. Nor, though she had yet to understand it, was the image of ice maiden.

When she stepped into the wine bar, the fug of alcohol fumes and cigarette smoke rushed to greet her, like a drunk at a party, wrapping itself around her, welcoming her with a winey kiss. Drink was the downfall of so many in her profession. Broken veins and bulbous noses were almost a badge of office among the raincoat army of Grub Street. Cassie, conscious of the debilitating effects, the brain-rot induced by booze, was careful to limit herself to the occasional glass of dry white wine.

Difficult, especially on a day like this when, though Christmas was still more than a week away, an atmosphere of rather desperate jollity prevailed. As she shouldered her way through the throng, workmates caught at her sleeve, asked her to join them, wanted to know what she would have.

'What's your poison, Cass?'

'Over here, Cassie.'

'A drink Miss Murray?'

'Phew, they're doing good business in here today!' she remarked as she reached John Stirling's side, and she tolerated the arm which he slid around her waist, for it was all part of the prevailing chumminess.

'A little livener?'

'The usual, please.'

When he had furnished her with a drink, he told her more about the bitter wrangle between Nick Moy and the Editor. 'Six of one and half a dozen of the other' was how he apportioned the blame. 'You know what Nick's like, the way he loses his rag over the slightest thing. And Ant's so stubborn, he won't be told he's wrong. Anyway, worry not about our old pal Moy. He'll be snapped up by the opposition before you can say El Vino's. Shouldn't wonder if he'd already had an offer, eh? Didn't want to work his six months' notice. Thought he'd force the issue.'

'I hope you're right, for Nick's sake.'

'Course I'm right. The *Inquirer*'s had its eye on our Nicko for a while. Editor snuggling up to him at cocktail parties, whispering sweet five-figure numbers in his shell-like. Well, every man has his price.'

'I suppose so,' Cassie agreed. 'Head-hunting', the practice of luring good journalists away from their employ with promises of fame and fortune, was rife in the competitive world of newspapers. The most visible writers, those whose stories appeared under a regular by-line, were naturally the most sought-after. It would be no great surprise if one of the rival Sundays had been courting Moy.

'What about Paul Roth?' she asked.

'What *about* him?'

'I mean, what's he like? As a person?' For while he was a writer of prodigious skill, it was rumoured that his talents lay in other directions too.

John confirmed it. 'A good guy. Bit arrogant at times, bit pushy, but he's all right. Clever, at least. I don't mind people being pushy when they've got it up here.' He tapped his brow with one finger. 'It's only when they're . . . you know, second-rate. Anyway, Paul has flair. Desperately attractive, too, curse him! Has every good-looking bird in the place making calf eyes at him. Boy, if I had his opportunities.' John's eyes glazed over as he considered this improbability.

'It's just as well you don't, I'd say,' Cassie told him wryly.

'That secretary of yours, Cass. The one with the . . . er . . .' John's hands described what mere words might fail to convey.

'Lorraine. What about her?'

'Got a boyfriend, has she? Going steady? Married or something like that?'

'No, but *you* are,' she admonished him with heavy irony, 'you're married ... or *something like that*.' In fact, she knew John to be very happy with his wife Glenys, a doting father to his teenage son and daughter, and doubted if he had ever actually been unfaithful beyond a little sexual adventuring of the imagination. All the same, she took no small delight in dousing his daydreams with cold water.

'Why must you remind me?' he groaned in mock anguish. 'Don't you know that's why I drink—to forget? Finished your wine, have you? Want another one for the road? Bar-tender, a glass of your best paint stripper over here, please.'

'Not for me thanks,' she intercepted the order. 'I'll buy you one, then I really must get back and finish my piece.' It mattered to Cassie that she should stand her round. If she'd been so disposed she could have spent every lunchtime eating and drinking with different men and never have to reach for her purse. But she was a firm believer in the saying that there is no free lunch: everything in life must be paid for somehow, some time.

'What-ho, is this a private party or can anyone join in?' Garry Schwarz from the Sports Desk made a timely appearance, proffering a bottle of the house red.

'Not private,' she said, 'but I'm just off.'

'And you, John?'

'Oh, I'm game.'

She left them to it, stepped out into the grey air, dodged the London traffic, the buses, lorries loaded with giant drums of paper, the fleets of delivery vans, the taxis shuttling management people to and from expense-account lunches, the motorbike messengers cutting in and out, dicing with death.

The noise and bustle made her feel very much alive, very much a part of the teeming world. And as she looked up at the *Monitor* offices, at the newspaper logo in four-foot-tall letters on the glass and concrete façade of the building, she felt a profound pride of achievement. This was where she had always wanted to be: she had made it!

When she entered the *In Touch* office she sensed a presence before she saw who was there. An occupied room is quite different from an empty one: a single being can fill the vacuum. She vaguely supposed it would be Bridie, back from reading proofs down with the printers, subbing on the stone. But no; a tall, male figure stood with his back to her, peering out at the grumbling machinery below.

'Can I help you?' she asked, for it was not a familiar back.

He turned to face her, and then of course she knew him. Knew who he was. The face was familiar after all; it had stared out at her from so many issues of the paper. 'Oh, hello, you're Paul Roth, aren't you?'

He was very tall—perhaps six-three, she thought—and slightly rangy. She judged him to be about thirty-three or four. He wore faded jeans, a leather flying-jacket with sheepskin collar turned up, and, with hands thrust deep into the pockets, he had a distinctly moody air about him. His brown-blond hair was awry, his brow was puckered, his expressive mouth drawn into a thin line, speaking silently of irascibility. He did not return the greeting or produce a hand from his pocket to offer it, but he perched on the edge of Lorraine's desk and glared around him. 'Since when has this been the *In Touch* office?' he demanded to know.

'Well, since ...' She was taken aback by such aggression. 'Since just after I came. When the section expanded to three pages. Nick Moy was happy to move. The *Prud'homme* office is down the corridor now, in Tim Pacey's old room. It's smaller, of course, but Nick actually preferred it. At least it's quiet down there, and gets a lot more natural light than we do.' She realised she was trying to justify the change-around, and wondered why she should feel obliged to do so. This was the office she had been allocated; it met her needs, if only just, and that was that.

'I see.' His gaze roamed, taking stock of the Christmas decorations, the fashion posters on the walls, the powdered milk and slimmer's biscuits on top of the stationery cupboard, the scented satin valentine heart which Lorraine had affixed to the noticeboard, and his mouth took a further downturn of distaste. He swung one long leg, drumming his booted heel against the metal wastepaper bin.

'They say you'll be taking over from Nick, is that right?'

'It's been suggested.'

Disdaining him, not willing to talk any more if he was not willing to be more civil, she went and sat at her desk, ran her eyes over the text that had been her morning's work, the story so far.

'I only just got back. I'm jet-lagged to hell.' It wasn't worded like an apology, it wasn't abject or even very gracious, but there was a conciliatory note in his voice now. 'To tell the truth, I don't know if I'm coming or going.'

'Would you like a cup of coffee?' she asked, relenting.

'That would be nice.' He gave a strained smile.

'Rather rude,' Cassie thought of him as she filled the kettle from the cloakroom tap. Straightening, she glimpsed her reflection in the mirror. Her hair was escaping from behind her ears, from the confinement of the slide, wisps of it framing her face. She set the kettle down, dragged back the rebellious locks, and then—without knowing why—unclasped the slide and let the dark tresses hang freely. Her nether lip looked dry and a little cracked. She moistened it with her tongue, drew her finger over it like a lipstick.

Yes, Paul Roth might be a gifted writer, but he was somewhat lacking in common courtesy.

'Is this you?' he asked her when she returned to the office. He was kneeling with one leg on her swivel chair and reading the page which curled out of the typewriter.

She wanted to snatch her copy away from his view. She was never very happy about it until it was finished, hated other people to see it until she had crafted the last sentence, and only really felt proud of it when it had been typeset, when it miraculously assumed real credibility.

'Is what me?' she asked tetchily.

'Are you Penny Dreadful?'

It was a pen-name she had dreamed up for her weekly column, in which she lampooned public figures with virulent wit. It had become a popular feature and generated a great deal of correspondence—not all of it favourable.

'I write it, yes. My real name is Cassie Murray, by the way.'

'Ah, of course, the Bright Young Thing! I've heard about you.'

'Good reports, I trust.'

'In the main.' He slapped at her copy with the back of his hand. 'It's entertaining stuff, but it could conflict with *Prud'homme*. If that's what I've been dragged back here to do, we shall have to take care not to tread on each other's toes.' By which he clearly meant, '*You* will have to take care not to tread on *my* toes.'

'Nick and I never found it a problem,' she told him icily, for it was a slight to her professionalism. 'There was always ample consultation. I really don't think you need to worry.'

She had to crawl under a table to plug the kettle in at the mains. When she emerged and, still kneeling, turned her head, she saw that he was staring at her and knew that he had been contemplating her shapely behind.

'Desperately attractive,' John Stirling had said of him. 'Has every good-looking bird in the place making calf-eyes at him.' Temper more than embarrassment coloured her cheeks. He'd better know—had Paul insolent Roth—that she was his colleague and his equal and would be treated as such.

Clatter went the metal spoon on the coffee jar. 'Milk? Sugar?' she asked snappily.

'Neither. I'll take it black. Might help to clear my head.'

'As you wish.'

The water boiled. Steam curled the corners of a
Liberty poster, a print of a girl in shepherdess garb, on
the wall. She made coffee, wondering why she was
showing civility to someone so patently uncivil.

'Thanks,' he said when she handed him one of the
matching floral mugs which Lorraine had chosen in another attempt to bring a touch of 'home' to the office.

'You're welcome.' She still felt miffy. 'I expect you'll
miss New York, won't you?'

'Sure I will.' He set the mug down on a letter which
Lorraine had carefully typed that morning. It left a wet
ring. 'And yet I'm not sorry to be back. I miss London,
too, when I'm away.'

'I suppose you must.' She returned to her seat, folded
her arms on the desk in front of her and rested the
weight of her upper body on them. She could think of
nothing more to say. Paul Roth was not the easiest
person with whom to make conversation.

He had a soft and slightly breathy voice which might
have been an affectation since it had about it that
whisper of sensuality, a bedroom undertone, and yet
something told her that it was natural. It had the effect
of making the listener incline towards him when he
spoke, making every word precious. It came to her that
he was indeed attractive. Not since her twentieth year
had any member of the opposite sex managed to rattle
her quite as he was doing. But then, she decided, that
might have more to do with his abominable rudeness
than with his strong, square face.

'You won the Margaret Thingummy Award, I
understand,' he husked at her. She thought perhaps
exhaustion was making his throat rasp. There were
charcoal smudges around his grey-green eyes, deep
vertical furrows in either cheek.

'The Marguerite Palfrey Award,' she corrected him.
It was a prize given annually to a promising new female
writer, and it carried no small cachet in the profession.
It had earned her six hundred pounds, a silver inkwell

and overnight success, since it was winning the award for a piece she had written in a women's weekly magazine that had brought her to the notice of Anthony Holt and landed her the job on the *Monitor*.

'Yes, that one. Good for you! Stroke of luck, eh? I guess it helped you to sneak into journalism by the back door.'

She slammed her mug down so hard that coffee leapt out and went splat on the desk. 'How dare you say that?' She felt a nerve twitch in her cheek, felt the colour drain out of her face, leaving her bloodless with rage. 'How dare you imply ... I've worked for everything I have; nobody ever handed me anything on a plate. I'm a *bona fide* journalist, just like you, and don't you ever forget it!'

'I only meant . . .' he replied, shaking his head, and as the red mists cleared she saw that he had actually intended no offence. 'Most of us come to Fleet Street through more arduous routes. Cub reporter on the *Croydon Advertiser*, that sort of thing. Trainees in the provinces. It seemed to me you had managed to cut through all that, come here more directly, that was all.'

For a moment he dropped his head and pressed his hands to his face. It was a gesture of utter weariness. Incongruously, she noticed that the wisps of hair at the back of his neck grew to his collar. It looked generally hacked about; she thought he was the sort of man who would take the scissors to it himself rather than bother with trendy hairdressers.

'All right,' she allowed rather grudgingly. Perhaps she had been a little too quick to anger? Was she, in fact, just a touch over-sensitive in such matters? And did it arise from the sense of inferiority which ran deep within her, beneath the surface confidence, causing her now and then to doubt her own credentials?

'Oh, my fault, I dare say.' He lifted his head and surprised her because, like a quick-change artist, a master of disguise, he was transformed: all trace of ill-humour had been erased, and the expression he wore now was positively pleasant. 'Look, I do hope we can be friends. No reason why not, eh?'

'No,' she heard herself agreeing, 'no reason at all.'

'Well ...' He stood up and took a swig of coffee, then set the mug down. 'I shall go and see if Ant is back in his office. See if he has anything up his sleeve for me, eh?'

'I'm sure he'll offer you Nick's old job,' she told him. 'I gather you're odds-on favourite for it.'

'I don't know if "offer" is the word,' he told her with a humorous chuckle. 'It will be more a case of, "Will you do the job or will you do the job?".'

'Not a matter of choice? But you'd like it anyway, wouldn't you?'

'Yes,' he told her frankly. 'Yes, I'd like it very much.'

'Then I hope you get it.'

'Thanks.'

She saw him to the door as she might a visitor to her home.

'We must have lunch,' he suggested. 'One day next week, perhaps? Get properly acquainted.' He waved one big hand around distractedly. 'When I get myself settled in again.'

'That would be nice,' she replied, and she thought maybe she meant it and was not merely being polite.

When he had gone, she turned to look in the mirror which Lorraine had placed on top of one of the filing-cabinets. Ice-maiden? Blue-stocking? Or just Plain Jane?

'You'll never guess what I just heard!' Bridie came bustling into the room wearing her usual Prince of Wales tartan skirt and air of dependability, flimsy sets of proofs, type-pulls fluttering from her hand like streamers in the draught from the door.

'No, don't tell me. Nick Moy's resigned?' Cassie, suppressing a smile, pretended to hazard wildly. So the story had reached the composing room, the 'shop floor', she thought.

'You heard already?'

'John Stirling told me.'

'They say the heir apparent for Nick's job is——'

'Paul Roth,' Cassie pre-empted Bridie again.

'That's right. He'll be on his way back from New York by now.'

'Not on his way. He's back already.'

'He is? That was fast work! How do'you know?'

'Because he was in here a few moments ago.' Cassie explained.

She rattled away at her typewriter for a few minutes. It was the way she wrote—in bursts, surges of inspiration causing her to work urgently for minutes between reflective pauses.

'Someone should tell Olinda Kington.'

'Who? Tell her what?' asked Cassie, preoccupied.

'Olinda Kington. You know she used to work here, I suppose?'

'Well, of course. She was on the News Desk, wasn't she, until she moved to bigger and better things? But what about her?' The formidable Ms Kington was a familiar face on television these days, an interviewer renowned for her provocative and tendentious line of questioning. But what had she to do with Paul Roth?

'Well . . .' Bridie began with a certain satisfaction (at last, a snippet that Cassie hadn't already heard!). 'She used to go out with Paul Roth, you know. It was the Big Romance of last year'—she stressed the words with a twinkle to imply the kind of overblown affair about which everyone would have been talking—'but they split up when he went to the States. Or before. Nobody really knew how it ended.'

'I hadn't heard that one.' For reasons she could not herself have explained, this information gave Cassie pause.

Bridie tapped the side of her nose with one finger. 'Rely on me to bring you all the scandal.'

'I do,' Cassie said with a laugh, and resumed her typing.

*   *   *

It was past eight o'clock when Cassie finally let herself into her small North London flat. As always she hesitated on the threshold and a little tremor of fear ran through her, causing the back of her scalp to prickle, as she listened for sounds of an intruder. It was not that she expected a burglar, but she still had a childish terror of the dark—terror, too, of what might be revealed when she snapped on the light.

She believed herself to be temperamentally suited to living alone. She had shared digs as a student, and for a while had taken a furnished room in a rented house in Streatham as she struggled to make a name for herself as a writer, but there had always been something—the noisiness or untidiness of a fellow inmate; tights steeping in the tub when she wanted to have a bath; no milk in the fridge for tea in the morning because someone had poured the lot over their cornflakes—to annoy her. Better peace and quiet, she had decided, even if that meant a degree of loneliness. Better to be able to lie soaking in your own bath without anyone hammering on the door. Better to be free to sit at the typewriter into the small hours without fear of disturbing the household.

Now she saw movement in the shadows and, after a heart-stopping instant, heard a welcoming mew. Her two cats, Paddy and Perkins, came to greet her with tails held high, to scrape and grovel at her feet.

'Hello, hello,' she laughed, stooping to stroke them, her whiskery friends, her only company. 'You want your dinner, do you? All right, I'll see to it. Though you might give me a moment to relax. It really has been one hell of a day.'

And it had. Anthony, in one of his picky moods, had found all kinds of fault with her pages just as they were due to go to press. He wanted a different treatment for this story, queried the veracity of that one. Cassie knew better than to argue with him: at times like this he must be humoured. Thank heavens Bridie had been there to help her sort things out, to suggest workable compromises and to put them into effect.

'I don't see what the problem is,' Cassie had confided to her miserably, feeling herself undermined.

'Och, take no notice of the stupid wee man!' Bridie had reassured her, unruffled. 'He's just blethering, never you worry.'

Cassie had known she was right. All the same, she felt the strain. And she had stayed late to read the final pulls, nervous that mistakes might have crept in when the changes were made.

All of which, of course, was a matter of total indifference to her furry friends, whose minds had turned, as one, to the prospect of food. Scolding them affectionately, she went to the bright little kitchen and found them some scraps before wondering what, if anything, she might herself eat.

There was some cheese in the fridge, some eggs. She might just whip up an omelette. Or she might take a bath, which was a miraculous way of unwinding, the water soft and scented with essential oils to soothe the body and promote a sense of well-being.

She switched on the television, and Olinda Kington's face appeared on the screen. She was attractive but a little hard-looking, with those pale blue eyes which had the glassy coldness of marbles, and those fine plucked eyebrows which she would raise in an eloquent expression of cynicism. Cassie had the unsettling notion that she had somehow conjured the image of the woman by thinking about her—mentioning her name— earlier that day, in the office. For a moment she paused to watch her perform—to see how she ran verbal rings around a spokesman for the Labour Party. She would be about thirty-two or thirty-three, Cassie thought, much the same age as Paul Roth. But an unlikely pair they would have made. She found it hard to imagine them together and, without asking herself why, but with a little tush of impatience, she snapped off the television and went to run her bath.

While the tub was filling, she changed into an old

towelling robe and put a record on the hi-fi, folk songs of the Auvergne, which never failed to ease her soul, evoking the passions of simple people, calling to mind the breathtaking beauty of the pastureland which lies between the rivers Loire and Dordogne in France. The soaring melody filled every corner of the flat; the windows shuddered in their frames with the loveliness of it.

Cassie was just lowering herself gratefully into the steaming water, feeling the tensions flow out of her, when the telephone rang, jangling her up again.

'Hello?' she spoke impatiently into the receiver, hugging a towel around her, dripping on the parquet floor.

'Hello, Cassie, is that you?'

'Yes. Is that Barbara?' For she instantly recognised the calm tones of Anthony Holt's implacable private secretary.

'Yes. Look, sorry, lovie, but something's cropped up. Anthony would like you back in the office. I'm sending an editorial car for you if it's convenient.'

'All right then.' Cassie knew well enough that, convenient or not, she had no option but to return to the office. The job must always come first.

'Be with you in about fifteen minutes.'

'I'll be ready.' Cassie inspected her fingernails. They were very short and square and businesslike: typist's fingernails. 'Any idea what it's about?'

'Oh, nothing too dramatic. Just a bit of a rethink.'

'See you, then.'

And Cassie went, shivering, back to the bathroom.

The December frost had patterned the windows with a delicate filigree. A biting wind nosed up the wastepipe. Thankfully she slid back into the water's warm embrace, to lie there, most of her submerged, just her head and shoulders, her breasts like small islands, breaking the surface. But she had little time. Reluctantly she clambered out again, wrapped herself in a huge white towel and went to stand in her bedroom next to the radiator, wisps of steam curling from her as she dried.

What to wear? For the clothes she had worn all day lay in a crumpled heap. She flung open the wardrobe door and surveyed the contents hanging there so orderly and laundered and fresh. Such sensible clothes, well tailored, made to last! An outfit for every occasion ... almost. The only glaring omission was a dress or blouse or skirt for more frivolous contingencies.

Cassie Murray was not a frivolous young lady.

With a sigh she pulled out a pair of black linen trousers and a cream blouse, and lined up black leather ankle boots, side by side, smartly to attention. She dropped the clothes on the bed and let the towel fall to the floor, turning to confront her reflection in the long mirror. She imagined it to be a secret, cunningly kept under wraps, this enchanting body of hers. As some women hope to conceal, disguise or play down lumps and bumps and folds, so she dressed to hide a figure of such impeccable proportions that she might have been a model had she stood taller than five-foot four. Or had she been so minded—which, of course, she was not.

Cassandra Murray had, for as long as she could remember, wanted to be a journalist. She had no idea when the seed of this ambition was first sown in her young mind, for it seemed to have been there germinating all her life.

Perhaps her name had had something to do with it. Her parents had chosen it because they liked the sound of it, but from an early age people had remarked on it, told her about the famed *Daily Mirror* columnist, the late William Connor, who wrote under the name of Cassandra.

If it had ever been an inspiration to her, however, she nowadays found it distinctly irksome, and went under the name of Cassie in the hope that people wouldn't continually pick up on it, telling her 'You're in the right job, then', or asking, 'You know about William Connor?' Besides, Cassie was a more wieldy handle, easier to manage.

When she had scrambled into her clothes she knelt on the floor to brush her hair, which was thick and velvety, but which crackled and drifted in the frosty atmosphere. She stroked mascara on her long, dark lashes, dabbed a hint of colour to her high cheekbones, a little smudge of shadow around her eyes. She never wore lipstick, disliking the brazen statement it made and the way it left its imprint on cups and glasses. Her make-up, like her clothes, was ever discreet.

When the doorbell rang, she hurried out, snatching up her coat. 'Hello Jack,' she said to the chauffeur. 'Filthy night.'

'A bit nippy, yes. Are you ready, then, Miss Murray?'

'Yes, let's go. Get it over with. Though I can't imagine what this is all about.'

'I couldn't say, Miss.'

It was a short ride by car, back to Fleet Street, now that the rush-hour traffic had subsided. As they sped along the frost-glazed roads, Cassie felt an increasing sense of *angst*. She had never been summoned in this fashion before, and could only guess at the reason for it.

Had she made some terrible error which had only now come to light? Had the libel lawyers raised a query? Might someone who featured on her pages have taken out an injunction to prevent publication? That seemed unlikely. Had they been served with a dreaded 'D notice' because the content of an article was a threat to national security? No, that was impossible.

She said a polite and distant 'Good evening' to the commissionaire as she hurried to the lift and ascended to the fourth floor. Inside, she was beginning to quake.

Her footsteps echoed the length of the corridor as she approached the editor's outer office, where Barbara sat smiling, shuffling papers.

'Go right in,' she told Cassie, and her expression betrayed nothing.

With trepidation, Cassie gave a token rap on Anthony Holt's door and pushed it open.

The editor was sitting there with Paul Roth. They had the aspect of a reception committee: there was the sense that they had been waiting for her. More than that, she somehow knew that she had been the subject of their discussions. 'Trouble,' said a voice in her head, ever more insistent. 'This means some kind of trouble.'

CHAPTER TWO

'Ah, there you are Cassie! Thanks for coming in at such short notice,' Anthony greeted her. 'Hope I haven't ruined your evening. Perhaps you had something else planned?'

'It's all right,' Cassie said, declining to reveal whether or not she had indeed got better things to do. The less you told your colleagues about your private life, in her view, the more they would respect you. And she had become adept at giving pleasant but oblique answers to direct questions.

'Help yourself to some coffee and sit down,' Anthony invited her. And, as she went to pour herself a cup of black, treacly, Continental brew from the Cona machine on the sill, 'I believe you've already met Paul Roth.'

'Yes, very briefly.' She turned and gave Roth a hello-again nod. He was sitting in one of the easy chairs at the far end of the room where Anthony Holt held his regular 'strategy meetings'. He looked more than merely relaxed: he was like a puppet whose strings had been cut. She guessed that he was by now so tired that he was in that state of semi-euphoria which follows unutterable weariness, when people's voices reach you as from a great distance, slightly drowned out by a ringing in your ears, and when nothing in the world seems to matter that much. It was a condition familiar to Cassie from the long hours she had sat at home working and reworking the text of her column in her over-anxious early days at the *Monitor*.

It was rumoured of Ant that he never slept at night, but stole ten-minute catnaps at intervals throughout the day, from which he awoke completely refreshed and mentally alert. She didn't know if this were true, but it would explain, she thought now, his total lack of consideration for a member of his staff who, after a transatlantic flight, and having exchanged morning for afternoon, daylight for night, was, figuratively speaking, dying on his feet.

On impulse, she handed the cup of coffee to Paul Roth and fetched another for herself.

'You're the first of the journalistic staff to hear the news, Cassie,' Anthony went on. 'Paul has come back to London to be *Prud'homme*.'

'Congratulations,' she said warmly, smiling at Roth, secretly amused by this 'revelation'. It was another of Ant's little quirks that he seemed oblivious of house gossip. And, considering that the business of a newspaper was the gathering and dissemination of information, such a blind spot in an editor was bizarre if rather endearing.

She sat down opposite Anthony and at right-angles to Roth. And it occurred to her to wonder why, out of everybody, she was the first to be told officially of the appointment.

'We'll be taking this opportunity,' the editor continued, 'to revamp the paper in some aspects. Have a bit of a rejig.'

Cassie felt a quickening of her pulses as she anticipated what came next, a hot rush of anger which coloured her cheeks. She knew before he outlined his ideas that this 'revamp' would have implications to her own section.

'We'll be moving *Prud'homme* towards the front of the Review section,' Anthony went on coolly, 'and we'll be introducing a new regular feature: a personality spot, a weekly interview with someone in the public eye. That's going to be Paul's baby. We'll call it something like The Paul Roth Profile or . . .' he paused, beamed, inviting Cassie to share his little joke '. . . The Grapes of Roth.'

She could barely manage a smile at this feeble witticism. She now knew for sure what was coming next. She glanced over at Paul Roth, who was watching her impassively, his strong, mobile face temporarily wiped clean of expression. Temper was like a collar about her neck, too tight, choking her.

'In Touch will be given a new look too,' Anthony explained, holding one manicured hand out in front of him, spreading the fingers, inspecting the fine webbing between them, the stretched folds of skin that showed red in the light of the Anglepoise lamp. 'We're going to have to tighten it up a bit. Squeeze it back into two pages. Make it more . . .' the hand became a fist, tight clenched, waving in the air, 'more punchy. More concise.'

Cassie had one very firm rule when it came to confrontation: she never showed she was upset. To cry, as she felt like doing at this moment, would be to let herself down. To be unprofessional. And it would allow the editor to dismiss her as an hysterical female. She fought to bring her galloping thoughts under firm control, took a deep breath and asked, 'Are you not happy with the section as it is?'

'My dear Cassie . . .' His tone was soothing, placatory and slightly patronising. 'I have the greatest admiration—we all do—for the way you run your pages. You really must believe that. It's simply that . . . we feel the time has come for a change. And something has to go. The suggestion is that you should reduce your fashion coverage, run shorter articles, that's all really. And . . . uh . . . we don't see a place for Penny Dreadful in the new scheme of things.'

It was as though a personal friend of hers had been summarily and ignominiously dismissed. Cassie felt pure outrage on Penny's behalf. Damn it, Anthony Holt had no right . . .

It was a bad decision, too. The Penny Dreadful column was liked by the readers, enjoyed—in most cases—even by those who had the dubious honour to feature in it.

'I'd sooner lose the fashion coverage altogether,' she ventured.

But it was not negotiable. It had already been

decided, she now saw, by these two men, Anthony Holt
and Paul Roth. All at once she was sure this was Roth's
doing. His idea. He wanted space in the paper—a much
sought-after and jealously protected commodity—to
gratify his ego and further his ambitions. He had almost
certainly made it a condition of acceptance of the
Prud'homme job. He'd been making demands and
Anthony—set now on having him back in London—
had meekly complied.

'I would remind you,' she said with the merest tremor
in her voice, drawing his attention to the most recent
readership figures, by which Anthony set much store,
'that almost fifty per cent of our audience are women,
and of those, eighty per cent read *In Touch* each week.'

Anthony's fingers played pianissimo on the edge of
the glass-topped table. 'Your section will immediately
follow *Prud'homme*,' he said after a strained moment.
'And the Paul Roth Profile will appear right after that.
Penny Dreadful would be too much of the same. And
there would be the danger of conflict or overlap. No,
what we need from you, Cassie, is a change of pace,
something altogether different.'

Slap went his hand now on the table, a gauntlet being
thrown down, a challenge to her journalistic skill and
ingenuity. The misty dabs left by his fingertips on the
glass dissolved slowly. As did her hopes of changing
Anthony's mind.

'There would be a danger of conflict'? Paul Roth had
said something similar earlier that day. Suggested that
she might run a story which would not sit happily in the
same issue as one of his. Suggested that she might 'tread
on his toes'. She was utterly convinced, now, that it was
he she must thank for all this.

'I know we can rely on you,' Anthony flattered her,
'to come up with a bright new formula for your spread.'

Her spread. Two facing pages. And this so soon after
they'd given her a third! It was all very, very
disappointing.

'Come and see me next week,' Anthony invited,

getting to his feet, opening his arms, indicating to both Cassie and Roth that the interview was over. 'Show me some ideas for the new *In Touch*. See if you can come up with something entirely original.'

'I'll do that,' she said as she allowed herself to be ushered to the door. She sensed Paul Roth behind her but did not look back as she walked through Barbara's deserted office and down the corridor, then out into the lobby where she called the lift.

She heard the tread of cowhide boots on the stone floor, heard him stifle a yawn. The lift arrived, and the doors rolled back and she stepped inside. Paul Roth stepped in beside her and she punched the button marked 'Ground'. Not a word passed between them.

The doors closed again, the lift juddered as it descended one floor, two . . . Then it stopped. 'Blast it!' muttered Cassie as she jabbed the button again to remind the stupid contraption what it was supposed to be about.

Still nothing happened.

She looked down at her feet, at her ankle boots, the butts of cigarettes and the spent matches which spilled from an ashtray under the 'No Smoking' sign and littered the floor. 'It's stuck!' she thought, and the tears which she'd been damming up began to sting her eyes. 'Oh, no, I can't believe this! The rotten lift has broken down!'

Paul Roth reached past her and in his turn pressed the button—pressed all the buttons—in the forlorn hope that the tinny vehicle would continue on its journey.

The atmosphere was suddenly intolerably tense: so much hostility in such a confined area. He had done her down terribly. Her most basic impulse was to hit out. She'd have liked to deliver a good kick to his shin or a slap to his face. But she must contain all her emotions, no matter what.

'The telephone,' he said, and she was struck again by the gruff, soft sensuality of his voice.

'Sorry?'

'There's a telephone. There, in that locker. For emergencies. Pick it up and dial the operator. They'll have to come and rescue us. Tell them to bring a tin-opener and get us out.'

A treacherous little giggle escaped her—in spite of the fact that she didn't feel one bit like laughing. She opened the metal locker door, took out the receiver, dialled. 'Hello? Switchboard? Look, it's Cassie Murray here. I'm stuck in the lift with ... with a colleague. Can you send for the engineers?'

'All right dear, I'll see to it,' came the motherly voice of the operator. Cassie imagined her as comfortable, middle-aged, doing her knitting even as she spoke.

'Will it take long?'

'I couldn't say, ducks. I'm sure they'll be as quick as they can.'

'All right then. Thanks.' She hung up and turned to relay this to Paul Roth. 'She said they'll be as quick as they can.'

The unkind light from a fluorescent strip bleached his face and accentuated the tiredness smudges around his eyes. She guessed that she, too, would have taken on a gaunt aspect. He lounged against the wall and then slid down to a sitting position. 'Might as well make yourself comfortable,' he suggested.

'Comfortable?' The laugh she uttered then was short and bitter. In such limited surroundings, and with the disappointment pressing in on her, hampering her breathing, comfort was the last thing she might hope for.

'I trust Anthony hasn't put your nose out of joint,' he said.

She declined to answer.

'I did admire your column. Like I said, it was good stuff. You write very well.'

Still she would not deign to reply. How could he be such a hypocrite? Or did he imagine she hadn't guessed that he was behind all the changes?

'But I'm sure you'll have no trouble coming up with a new formula for your section. It's probably time for a change in any case.'

Now she turned to glare down at him where he sat with his knees apart, his hands thrust into his jacket pockets, and for the second time caught him in the act of sizing her up, assessing her charms. The frank, unguarded sexual interest in his eyes found response deep within her as some unconforming part of her, some maverick impulse, heedless of her rational mind, was sparked like a flint struck against stone.

'Where the hell are the engineers?' she asked tetchily.

'Give them a chance. You only just sent out the SOS. You know you can't hurry things round here. I once waited nine months to get my typewriter repaired.'

'That's different. This is an emergency. They ought to be more concerned about us.'

He yawned again and slumped further down, still subjecting her to rather insolent scrutiny. 'Why don't you come and sit here by me? We could get better acquainted.'

'No, thank you.'

'Look, Cassie, I know you're feeling sore, but it's really just one of those things. You shouldn't take it personally.'

'*You* wouldn't take it personally, I suppose. If someone took away one of your pages. Made you drop your column. Killed it just like that!' She snapped her fingers at him. 'I suppose you'd simply shrug your shoulders, would you, and tell yourself that it was just one of those things?'

'Watch it, kid,' he told her, 'your inexperience is showing.'

'I don't see what it has to do with inexperience. I'm upset, of course I am. I'm also bloody livid. I worked long and hard to establish that section. When we were allocated the extra page, it was in recognition of that fact. I'd earned it, that's all. Then you come breezing back, making your demands, grabbing what you can, taking advantage of the situation, taking it for all it's worth. My God, they told me you were arrogant and pushy, but I had no idea how much!'

'And they told *me* you were a little swot. A worker. A grafter. Very serious, they said. Very *dedicated*.' On his lips it sounded like a slur.

'Oh, I see. You've been making enquiries about me already!'

'And you about me,' he countered with a mischievous grin.

She would not relent, would not unbend. 'Naturally you've been the subject of some discussion in the past twenty-four hours. I just happened to hear a thing or two.'

'Well, I don't mind admitting I did ask a few questions about Cassandra Murray,' he allowed.

'*Cassie*,' she corrected him.

'Cassie then. Though I like the sound of Cassandra. Good name for a journalist. You've heard of William Connor, I suppose? Oh, sorry, yes, I see you have. I suppose everyone says that to you?'

'Not everyone,' she informed him, her tone laced with sarcasm. 'Some people aren't that crass.'

'Yes, well,' he went on, 'I asked this and that about the prissy young woman with the neat little bum and the fathomless brown eyes.'

Prissy? Or had he said 'pretty'? She wasn't sure. 'What *exactly* did you want to know about her?'

'Oh ...' His eyes travelled over her with the thoroughness of a forensic expert dusting for prints. He affected building-site coarseness as he told her, 'Usual sort of questions, you know. Who gets to bed her? What's she like in the sack?'

She knew he was sending her up, but she wasn't sure at what level, and had no idea why. What point was he trying to make? Irritation made her face and neck prickle. 'And what did you learn?' she asked acidly.

'Very little. It seems you're something of an enigma.'

'Perhaps because I happen to think,' she sermonised,

'that one's private life should be precisely that.' This rather high-and-mighty statement concealed a depressing truth, a fact which she could not altogether escape—which was that she had no private life worth talking about, and no love life whatever.

He seemed, somehow, to guess it. To be able to see right into her mind. 'It strikes me,' he said, 'you're rather too buttoned up.' And he wasn't referring to the pearly buttons which held her blouse closed across her bosom.

"It strikes me,' she came back at him, 'that you've got the most appalling cheek to talk that way.'

'I confess I was curious to meet you. Keen to.' He tried seriously to explain. 'I'd been reading what you wrote and I formed a mental picture of you and I wanted to see if you measured up to my imagining.'

'And do I?'

'In some regards.'

'Such as?'

'Well, I expected you to be attractive—though perhaps not *as* attractive.'

She made a dismissive little tutting noise. What had looks to do with anything?

'But I'd visualised a more sparkling personality, someone socially at ease, lots of charm.'

'And you find me lacking in it?'

'I think Miss Murray, that I discern a flicker of light under a bushel. I think you suppress a lot of things. I say again, you're all buttoned up.'

'Oh, you do?'

'I do. And I have this almost irresistible urge to unbutton you.'

And now, it seemed, he *was* referring to actual buttons, to clothing. He wanted to discover the secret her, the body beneath the somewhat severe garments rather than the person behind the façade—although perhaps, in exploring one, he would come unawares upon the other.

'I had heard,' she sneered, 'that you liked your women to be . . . up front. High profile.'

'You'd heard that, had you?'

'Ladies like Olinda Kington.'

Now it was his turn to look annoyed. It showed for just a moment in his face, anger tugging at his brow, darkening his eyes. But he continued in light-hearted vein, 'So the Great Gossip Machine is still working efficiently as ever here?'

'It would seem to be.' It occurred to her that she had, without really meaning to, scored a bullseye. The sharp little dart, tipped with poison, had hit the mark. Olinda Kington was indeed his ideal woman. Perhaps he was still a bit in love with her. Maybe she had ditched him—and that would have been hard for a man like Roth, who had almost certainly been used to having his pick of girlfriends.

The sudden surge of anger from him lent an extra charge to the atmosphere, which his dismissive words did not dispel. Cassie was acutely conscious of every breath she drew, felt the passage of air through her nostrils right down into her gasping lungs.

'I don't know if one is really always attracted to types,' Paul Roth said. 'In fact, my tastes are wide-ranging—in the opposite sex as in everything.'

For uncounted moments, silence settled on them. Paul Roth flexed his fingers, giving a clue to inner tensions. Then, 'Sit down, Cassie,' he said, and the weariness was back, the throatiness. 'Here.' He ripped off his jacket and spread it out for her on the dusty lino floor of the lift. 'You might as well take the weight off your feet. They may be a while yet.'

It would have been hard to refuse. She sat on the sheepskin-lined jacket which he had so gallantly offered. 'What can be keeping them? Surely they won't be much longer?'

'I don't suppose so. Meanwhile, what shall we do to pass the time?'

Sitting by him, she found herself frighteningly sensitive to his masculinity, aware of the movements of his hands, the trespass of his gaze upon the secret regions of her body, of her being.

'We could play I-spy,' she suggested.

'Not many possibilities here.'

'You have a better idea?'

The look he gave her plainly told her that he *had*. More sparks cascaded inside her, a sizzling heat which subsided almost at once, leaving her ice-cold across her shoulders, causing her to shiver. She told herself that she was not attracted to him—that these physical reactions were merely symptoms of the fury she felt, or the onset of a bout of flu.

But he had somehow breached the barriers of chill respectability which she had years ago erected. He was over them, on the inside, with her, where she was reachable and touchable and vulnerable.

'All right.' He straightened his legs out in front of him, lounged there allowing his gaze to dance over her. 'I spy with my little eye, something beginning wi-ith . . .'

He advanced one hand and took hold of her blouse, where facing turned into collar, tugged gently at the fabric with one hand. She felt her eyes open wide but she made no move to resist. In these extraordinary circumstances, it suddenly seemed to her, the extraordinary might happen. They were trapped there, suspended between floors—suspended, as it might be, in time and space. And whatever they did would be separate from and somehow *outside* reality.

The pearl buttons put up token resistance, then she felt the fabric part, felt cold air to her skin. Looking down she saw with some surprise that she was exposed to the waistband, that he had revealed a long 'V' of flesh, the cleft between her breasts, the gentle swell to right and left which his venturesome hand went in search of.

She never wore a brassière, preferring to be unfettered. Now she felt shameless, wanton—and she didn't even care.

Once before, she had lost her head in this way—and, consequent upon it, had lost her heart. That had not been a happy experience. She'd vowed it would never happen again. And yet, here she was, with a virtual stranger, someone whom she didn't even *like*, in such improbable surroundings. 'It's so sordid here,' she told herself, and that very thought was peculiarly arousing.

Slowly, stiffly, he got to his knees in front of her, slid both hands under her blouse, gripped her not roughly but firmly, brought his mouth close to hers so she felt the warm moisture of his breath. His face was a wooden door upon which desire was battering: she could see how it pounded on the inside, 'Let me out, let me out!'

It was she who shouted it. And now she was on her feet, hammering at the door of the lift, yelling to be rescued from this imprisonment, saved from this man— or from herself.

'Don't panic,' he told her tersely, still kneeling, making no move to restrain her. 'They'll be here in a minute. Tidy yourself up.'

And, as she fell silent, as she buttoned her blouse and tucked it in, fastening her jacket over it, she heard him say, 'There's no chance that I shall have my evil way with you. I don't even want to. Not here, now, like this. That wasn't how I planned it.'

Planned it? Planned *what*? Part of her believed in the possibility that a mysterious electromagnetic force, such as sets planet on collision course with planet, might throw two people together against their very reason. For an instant she had felt a pull, an irresistible attraction to Paul Roth. But he was talking now about some kind of scheme, some grand design, of which she was the object.

All at once she perceived herself as prey. Tender quarry. How nearly she had fallen into his clutches! She felt frightened and appalled. And when the telephone in the little metal cupboard shrilled, she gave a violent start.

'Are you in there, Miss Murray?' asked a male voice, solid and reassuring over the crackling line when she put the receiver to her ear.

'Yes, of course I am.' Who did he think she was, Harry Houdini?

'All right then, are you? There's nothing to worry about. We'll have you out of there in a jiffy,' the owner of the voice, one of the maintenance staff, assured her.

Magically, as he spoke, the lift gave a little jolt and went wheezing down the shaft, the doors rolling back as they made welcome contact with the ground floor.

'Phew!' thought Cassie as she stepped out into the foyer, to see a man in white overalls coming down the stairs, spanner in hand.

'There you are then!' he said cheerfully. 'And none the worse for your ordeal, I trust?'

'No, none the worse.' She offered him a grateful smile.

'Well, then, I'll wish you good night, Miss Murray.'

'Yes, good night.'

It was inky blue beyond the glass doors. Cars and buses trundled by, throwing cones of light before them. Glancing at the clock above the reception desk, she saw it was nearly ten.

'I'll give you a lift home,' she heard Paul Roth say, close to her ear and in the hearing of the commissionaire. 'You won't find it easy to get a taxi out there and it's bitterly cold.'

'You have a car?' was all she could think to reply. In one way she was loath to accept the offer, would have preferred to get away from him as fast as she could. But it was freezing out, she might indeed face a long wait for a bus or cab, and it might not be a bad idea, anyway, to set the relationship with Roth back on a proper footing, to normalise it as far as possible.

'A company one,' he told her, holding the door open for her, nodding to the commissionaire by way of a good night. 'A little perk that goes with being *Prud'homme*.'

'You have done nicely for yourself!' she remarked nastily, remembering all the anger, the detestation that had been kindled in her during their brief meeting with Anthony Holt.

He gave her a sideways look of reproof which

eloquently told her not to be so childish or so obvious.
And he began to walk on ahead, so she found she had
to trot to keep up with him.

It was starting to sleet; freezing needles showed up in
the glare of headlights. When Paul turned to see if she
was with him, the wind slapped his collar against his
face.

The *Monitor* hierarchy, executives and very senior
journalists, were allowed to garage their vehicles in a
subterranean car park, an echoey vault which stank of
exhaust fumes and which rang with their hurried
footsteps as they descended the ramp and crossed the
bleak expanse of concrete to where a white car stood
waiting.

'Hop in.' Roth unlocked the passenger door before
going around to the driver's side. The interior smelt
damp and plasticky and Cassie, feeling cold to the
bone, clambered in and sat hugging herself.

Paul Roth got in beside her and adjusted the rear-
view mirror. He released a catch and slid the driving-
seat back as far as it would go to accommodate his long
legs. In profile he was extraordinarily handsome, for his
features were finely proportioned, clean of line; chin,
nose, cheekbones beautifully moulded; curiously light
eyes overshadowed by dark brows.

'Where to, then?' he asked, his breath vaporising, and
he dabbed at the windscreen as it began to mist over.

'Oh ... if you could just drop me at the tube. Any
station on the Northern Line.' For she had a sudden
horror of letting him drive her all the way, of giving
him a glimpse of where she lived and how.

'Don't be crazy,' he scolded her. 'The subway is no
place for a woman alone at night.'

The Americanism made her smile fleetingly. 'This
isn't New York,' she reminded him. 'London is still a
relatively safe place, you know. I don't expect I shall be
mugged or ... or attacked or anything.'

'Why chance it?' He turned the ignition key and the
motor started.

'I dare say I can look after myself.'

She found herself once again the object of his searching gaze. 'I dare say you can,' he agreed after a measured pause, and the words carried some import which she could not grasp.

'All right then, if you go up Farringdon Road, I'll direct you from there.'

It took a while for the engine to warm up, but then the heater started to work, hot air filling the car, making Cassie feel strangely cosy, cocooned. The scene beyond the windows took on the charming, fairyland aspect of a snowstorm ball.

'Have you eaten tonight?' he asked suddenly.

'Eaten?'

'Yes, you know. Dinner.'

In fact she'd had nothing since breakfast—and it hadn't occurred to her to feel hungry. On press days she lived very much on her nerves, and food was usually far from her thoughts. 'Well, no, I haven't actually.'

'Would you like to go for a meal somewhere? Keep me company? I'd appreciate it.'

It was a perfectly civilised proposition, a cordial invitation put to her with a hint of deference. She would have found it hard to refuse him. It was as though nothing had happened between them—as though the episode in the lift, their short-lived intimacy, had never been. She almost persuaded herself that she had dreamt it—that it had been the mere invention of her mind. Or perhaps the two of them had borrowed a few moments out of time, which need never afterwards be repaid, but which had simply now been written off.

'If you like,' she heard herself agreeing. 'That would be nice.'

'Where would you like to go? What d'you fancy? I'm a bit out of touch with the London restaurant scene.'

'There's an Italian place near me,' she said. 'It's not at all posh or trendy or anything, but the food's good. How would that do?'

'It would do just fine.' He bestowed upon her a smile

so dazzling that she could not but respond. She wanted to dislike him, that was the only reaction that made any sense. But he was a surprising personality, mercurial, changing so much from one instant to the next that it was difficult to isolate what it was about him that she might abhor.

'Trendy I don't need,' he informed her. 'Not the way I feel. I don't have the slighest inclination to rub shoulders with the Beautiful People tonight.'

'But you're going to have to,' she observed. 'That will be part of the job of gossip columnist, going among the glitterati.'

'Oh, I dare say I shall be able to cope,' he assured her drily. 'I do have a few social graces, you know. I have a grounding in social mores. I don't eat peas off my knife or blow on my soup, honest, Miss Murray, you could take me anywhere.'

He was taking the rise out of her again, but not unkindly, only teasing, reminding her that he was, after all, a man of the world.

'And you'll be on your best behaviour? You promise?' she joined in the joke.

'Scout's honour. Which way now?' For they were approaching a junction.

'Left, and then immediately right.'

Ten minutes later they drew up outside the friendly little trattoria which was Cassie's 'local', and where she ate sometimes with girlfriends or with her cousin Nicola when she was in town.

Pinello's was a scruffy little place, with the sort of dim-lit, comfortable atmosphere which people call 'intimate'. It was, by London standards, rather old-fashioned, with its clusters of Chianti bottles, candles on check-clothed tables, and all kinds of knick-knackery adorning the walls. The vogue these days was for pristine simplicity, pastel colours and chrome, or white walls and terracotta tiles, fans and ferns. The smart set would not be found any more, tangling with steaming plates of spaghetti, but preferred to toy, as was considered stylish, with itty-bitty dishes owing more to design than to culinary skill.

Cassie found herself hoping that Paul Roth would not disdain the slight shabbiness here, or the gargantuan portions. She need not have worried. 'Great!' he enthused as they stepped inside. 'Makes you feel ravenous, doesn't it?' For the air was redolent of the rich aroma of garlic and herbs.

'It does rather,' she agreed.

Pinello himself came bustling out to greet them, to beam a welcome and usher them to a table. He was a little barrel of a man with a perky moustache and a natty bow-tie. 'Hello, hello, good to see you,' he said, and, as he looked from Cassie to Paul, then back to Cassie, she knew that he was wondering if she had at last found herself a man—for he had never seen her in the company of an *inamorato*, a boyfriend, and, she was aware, considered this a criminal waste. These young people, these English, seemed to care so little for the good things in life, the sensuous pleasures, for food and drink and love!

How was she keeping, was it not cold for the time of year, where would she be spending Christmas ...? Pinello ran through the customary catalogue of questions, of restaurateur's small talk, while his eyes sought a more important answer: was the *bella signorina* at last planning to get down to that most worthwhile business of marriage and children?

'Would you like some wine?' Paul asked her, and something in his voice or in his look seemed to confirm what Pinello suspected.

Now his smile threatened to split his face, seeming to stretch almost literally from ear to ear. 'I get you some,' he told them, 'on the house. For Christmas.' And he hurried away to return with a bottle of Chianti Classico, which was ruby red and which tasted of Tuscan sunshine, with that curious, distinctive hint of oranges.

'Thank you very much,' Cassie smiled at him as she took a drink.

Paul swilled the wine in his glass, breathing the scent of it and, as Pinello bustled off to the kitchen, raised it to her in a toast, saying nothing, but taking a satisfied swig.

'Do you have far to go afterwards?' she asked him. 'Do you have your own flat or something?'

'Or something,' he said by way of reply. 'I have a house in Hackney. I bought it before I was sent to the States. I was going to do it up but there was a drastic change of plans. A friend has been living there and looking after it for me while I've been away.'

She wondered what he meant by 'drastic change of plans'. He might have been referring to his posting to New York, but she somehow felt he meant something closer to home, something altogether more domestic.

Had he bought the house to live in with Olinda Kington? Perhaps they had even planned to marry? Then she must have ditched him (Cassie had already persuaded herself that it was this way about), leaving him with a vast liability, an encumbrance of bricks and mortar. 'Will you sell it?' she asked.

The question seemed to surprise him. But then, he could not have known where her train of thought had taken her. 'Good heavens, no! It's my ideal house. I'm looking forward to living in it. Though it was early summer when I last saw it and there were roses growing under the front bay and sunlight streaming in. I should think it would be a bit different in winter.'

'It sounds lovely.'

'Well, it is. It's Georgian, four storeys, lots of stairs, and it's in a lovely square, all grass and almond trees out the front, and a secluded garden at the back.'

'Lucky you!'

'I shall be rattling around there on my own. It's really a family house, I suppose. The people who had it before had lots of kids. The basement is done out with a playroom.'

Cassie, thoughtful, took another sip of wine. His

plans had run to this, then: to having children with
Olinda! How very disappointing for him!

'I plan to have my study down there,' he told her
brightly, challenging all her notions of secret heartbreak,
of private disillusion. 'There's french windows giving
out on to a terrace, it's not the least bit dark or damp
or anything.'

'It must be nice to have a garden,' she said,
considering, thinking most of all that it would be good
for her cats.

'Gives you a sense of freedom. You can feel a bit
cooped up in a flat.'

'You can indeed.'

'Anyway ...' He seized a bread roll and pulled it
apart, broke himself off a mouthful. 'Let's eat, shall we?
What do you recommend?'

'Don't ask me, ask Pinello. He can tell you what's
best today.'

Ah, yes, the rotund proprietor informed them
proudly, they must try his Maria's *pollo con peperoni*,
which they duly ordered, causing him to glow with
pleasure. They would find it, he assured them,
magnifico. *Bello*. His thumb and index finger described
a circle, signifying perfection.

Nor were they disappointed. For the chicken
arrived, stewed with green, red and yellow peppers,
glistening with olive oil, sizzling in its earthenware dish,
smelling of onions and tomatoes, garlic, marjoram,
sweet basil and thyme.

Slight as she was, Cassie's appetite was quickly sated,
and she had reluctantly to lay her fork down before the
food was half eaten.

Paul Roth, who had demolished his swiftly and
neatly, began then to eat from her plate, talking all the
while, amusingly, about New York, about the newspaper business, about the arts and literature, revealing
that he was an educated and a cultured man, though his
style might be that of the more earthy pleasure-seeker.
Cassie, sitting back in the chair, derived obscure

pleasure from seeing him forking up what she had left. It was curiously intimate, strangely familiar, it made her feel surprisingly close to him. Lovers might share food. And good friends. It implied a certain mutual trust, an attraction.

But what was she thinking? The wine must be getting to her, making her mellow. She quickly, very consciously, ran through in her mind all the things she disliked about arrogant, pushy, grabby Roth.

When she felt his foot touch hers under the table, she jumped with shock and surprise. It was no accidental contact but a purposeful pressure. Raising her eyes to his, she saw that it was back—the hungry look, the pent-up desire moving behind his eyes like a figure at a window.

Abruptly she drew her feet under her, out of his reach. 'Do you want anything else? Some coffee? Or shall we go?'

'I'm easy. We can leave if you like.'

His tone was casual, untroubled. Perhaps, then, after all, the touch of his foot had been unintentional? Perhaps he had merely been flexing his legs to relieve the stiffness?

As she reached for her handbag he told her, 'I'll get this.'

'No, you mustn't. You don't have to treat me.'

An expression of sheer annoyance settled on his face. 'What's with you anyway? *I* asked you to have dinner. Can't you just be gracious and let me pay the bill?'

'Well, I ...' She was accustomed to men remonstrating with her—'No, no, I insist'—but this was different. Paul Roth was angry, he was telling her off like a naughty girl, trying to slap her down. 'I don't see why we can't go Dutch,' she said, and she was surprised to hear a peevish note in her own voice.

'All right then, have it *your* way.' He sat back, narrowed his eyes. '*You* pay, go ahead. If it makes you feel better.'

'It's not that it ...' She suddenly felt the need to explain. 'It's only that ...'

'I know exactly what it is, Cassie,' he informed her coldly. 'I've got your number, don't you worry.'

'You have?' she sneered at him, thrusting her chin out.

'You bet I do. You've got it in for men. You, Mistress Murray, want to emasculate any man you perceive as a threat.'

She flinched at this attack, her head whipping back as though he had hit her.

'I reckon you've been badly hurt some time by a guy.'

'Oh, do you?'

'Sure I do.' Suddenly, and with the speed of a cobra, he seized hold of her wrist. 'I'm right, aren't I? And you're out for revenge?'

'Let go, please. You're hurting me.' She blinked away the tears which started in her eyes.

'Own up. Tell the truth. That's your problem, isn't it?'

'If you say so,' she concurred with heavy irony. '*You're* the psychologist, apparently.'

'I don't need to be a psychologist,' he said, 'to read you. You're an open book.'

She shook him off and took her wallet from her bag. 'Pinello,' she said, raising her voice, managing, with a great effort of will, to sound cool and composed, 'could we have our bill, please?'

The friendly retaurateur brought the slip of paper, hesitating at the table, not sure to whom he should hand it. Paul Roth folded his arms in front of him and watched, disdainful, as Cassie held out her hand for it, ran her eye over it, counted out the crisp bank notes.

Through a door at the back of the restaurant came Pinello's wife, Maria. She was carrying a child in her maternal arms, a beautiful boy of about three, his head lolling on her shoulder, his thumb jammed in his soft, infant mouth, his slippered feet dangling. 'Antonio was having a nightmare,' she explained. 'He says he was dreaming about dragons. I don't know where they get these ideas.'

Paternal, loving, Pinello reached for his son, took the

sleepy bundle from his wife and cuddled him. 'He's our youngest,' he said, and he and Maria shared a look which spoke touchingly of pride of achievement.

The boy's eyes, fringed with impossibly long, dark lashes, opened, closed, opened. 'Is it nearly Christmas?' he asked engagingly, conversationally. And, on being told that, yes, it was, he instantly fell asleep again.

'Isn't he sweet?' said Cassie, feeling something move inside her, the stirrings of love and fierce protectiveness.

The tenderness of the moment, the open affection between Pinello and Maria, affected her. She was simply not angry any more. 'We have to be going,' she said. 'That was a lovely meal, Maria.'

'You like it?'

'Terrific,' Paul Roth told her expansively, and he stood up, stood tall, broad shouldered. 'Come on, Cass, where's your coat? We must make tracks.'

In the car she heard herself saying, 'I'm sorry.'

'Sorry?'

'For being . . . well, hostile.'

'And I'm sorry if I spoke out of turn. It's really none of my business.'

'No, it really isn't.'

'But, as I told you, I'm . . . Oh, the hell with it! Let's forget it.'

'I think that would be best.'

'Right you are. Where do we go from here?' And he meant geographically rather than in their relationship.

Outside the house where Cassie lived, he switched off the engine. 'Ask me in for coffee,' he said. And, reading mistrust in her eyes, 'Don't worry, I mean just that. A cup of coffee. It will keep me going until I get home. Don't worry, I'm not going to make a pass.'

'I didn't imagine that you were,' she said huffily, though in truth it had crossed her mind.

She went ahead of him to open the front door, led the way up the stairs and unlocked her own interior door. Reached for the light . . . 'Make yourself comfortable. I'll put the kettle on.'

And she left him sitting on the sofa as she went through to her bright little kitchen. She ground a handful of Blue Mountain coffee beans and tipped them into the jug, pouring boiling water on so that the grounds released their dark aroma. She took milk from the fridge, hunted vainly for sugar but found none. Still, maybe he didn't take it?

When she carried the tray through and set it down on the floor, she saw that tiredness had finally overtaken him.

Paul Roth was stretched out on her sofa, so deep asleep that it would have taken an earthquake to wake him.

CHAPTER THREE

THERE is a state between sleeping and waking when the dream world and the real world meet and merge, when the conscious and subconscious trade ideas, and when we are at our most imaginative and receptive, willing to entertain the bizarre, to believe anything possible. Lying in bed, drifting in and out of slumber, wandering in the borderlands of the mind, Cassie felt blissfully relaxed, aware of her body in its entirety, of the touch of the sheets against her silken skin. Her limbs felt melting, liquid, and she wasn't sure if her muscles would respond to the commands of her brain.

She knew that she was beautiful. Knew it because she felt it. Because she was open, for a while, to that concept. She knew that she had a flawless complexion, that her soft hair framed a near-perfect face, that she was slight of frame and sublimely proportioned. For a change she did not care to deny it.

But what was she without love? What good this face, what good this body? What good these arms if they had no one to embrace? What good these eyes if they had no one special person to behold?

In the daytime, through her hectic round, she might deny she had such basic needs, persuade herself that she was sufficient unto herself. And, by keeping busy, busy, she created an illusion of fulfilment. She fooled a lot of people, she half-succeeded in persuading herself. But her secret heart would always know the truth.

One moment there were hosts of dream-people around her—she saw them and heard their voices—and the next there was just one man, a *real* man, flesh and blood, standing over her.

Fanciful, she saw him as a Roman god, tall and bronzed and statuesque, with a corona of fair hair, wearing a toga.

Then she knew he was her visitor, her uninvited guest, Paul Roth, whom she had covered with a blanket and left to sleep on her sofa because it would have seemed so cruel to wake him.

He had a white bath towel about him. 'Move over, Cassie,' he said, and his voice seemed to issue from deep in his throat, resonant with contained passion.

Obedient, she shifted a little. Accepting, she waited for him to get in beside her, watched as he unswathed the towel and dropped it, negligently, on the floor.

It was awesome, really, the human body. A living miracle. She wondered at the hardness of knees, elbows, ribs, pelvis, the frame on which warm flesh was built. He must have bathed, for he was damp and soapy-smelling, though there was about him, too, a subtle, pleasing male scent.

'I want you,' he murmured, his breath warm in her ear, fanning her cheek, disturbing the little wisps of hair which clung there. 'I'm mad for you, Cassie. I'm sorry, I'm sorry. I have to make love to you.'

It was all perfectly natural, of course. The thing, above all else, which men and women were put on this earth to do. Making love was as right as rainfall and sunshine. It was lovely as the flowers.

She was herself a flower, opening to the daylight. Or she was a seashell, pink and cochleate, home to some pulpy, pulsing marine life-form. She was a cave, dark and undiscovered, waiting as the tide rose for the sudden salt inrush . . .

The hair of his head, slightly coarse, brushed her chin as his lips explored the territories of her throat, her shoulders, travelling downwards . . .

She heard him dredge the air from his lungs. Instinctively her fingers locked into his haunches, clawed at his back, held fast to him. Such anguish he seemed to be suffering, such a delicious torment. He uttered a groan and she answered it as he imposed his full weight upon her. There was no part of her which did not seem to fascinate him. He nipped the crook of her elbow, smoothed his face against her wrist . . .

There was one thing only, now, she wanted—to be united with him, unified, body with body, being with being.

'Please . . .' she said, meaning nothing by it if not 'Please go on.'

In her life she'd never felt like this—never been so committed, physically, mentally, to one end.

But there had been a time, years ago, when she had succumbed to the urgent demands of the male animal—to the persuasive, lying whispers of a man.

Gwyn, his name was, a poet, a dreamer—and how beguilingly he could mix word with word to express sentiments of love! She'd fallen for the line he'd spun her, fallen for his dark, brooding good looks, allowed herself to believe his extravagant declarations of undying passion.

Too late she'd learned that the thrill, for a man like Gwyn, was in the chase. Too late she'd seen him in the role of faithless seducer. Too late to save her heart from damage.

She'd been younger then, of course, and greener. Inexperienced. But what had experience taught her, after all, except distrust? She'd not acquired the trick of winning and keeping a man—rather she'd committed to memory the lesson never again to let one near her.

'I must possess you,' a husky voice said, and the words had about them the faint, distorted ring of an echo, seeming to reach her over a misty vale of years, reverberating back from past to present.

'I must possess you,' Gwyn had said to her—and once he had taken her he'd had no further use for her.

'Get away from me! Leave me alone!' All at once Cassie was galvanised by rage. Blind fury gave her extraordinary strength: with the flat of her hands she jacked him off her, causing him to roll on to his back.

Threshing with her arms and legs against the restraints of tangled sheets, she leapt out of bed and stood there, quivering with loathing. In an instant she

realised she was naked, and she snatched up the towel
which Paul had let fall by the bed, holding it in front of
her to hide herself from his gaze.

Bewilderment patterned his face, a confused frown
which hardened into an expression of cold contempt.
'So that's it!' He shook his head—shook it violently. 'So
that's your game! And I thought ... Ah, but I should
have known. Should have guessed. This is your idea of
revenge, isn't it? Your way of paying me back for the
bad turn you imagine I did you yesterday.'

He got to his feet and squared up to her, not the least
embarrassed, a man on good terms with his physique,
at ease with his own sexuality.

Miserably Cassie averted her gaze. 'I hadn't
meant...'

'I know just what you meant.' He took a step
towards her and she shrank back for all the world as
though she expected him to strike her.

'For God's sake!' he shouted in exasperation. 'Don't
behave like a scared cat. I'm not going to touch you.
Not again.'

'I never asked you,' she protested. 'I never invited
you to stay here, let alone to come into my bed.'

'You could have said no,' he pointed out, curling his
lip. 'You didn't have to play along. But you saw a
chance to humiliate me and you took it.'

'Oh, you just don't understand,' she wailed, and she
turned her back, sank down on the bed and doubled
over with misery, pressing the towel to her face. 'I'm
not vindictive,' she mumbled, 'that's not my way.
You're dead right, I think you've done me a rotten
turn, but I had no thought of repaying you. I hope I'm
big enough to rise above it.'

She was addressing an empty room, talking to no
one. She heard him down the passage, in the living-
room, grabbing up his clothes—heard the loose change
shower from his pocket, coins rolling about the floor.
He muttered an oath—coarse words which made her
flinch.

Presently came the jingle of car keys. His heavy tread towards the door. For Cassie it brought a sense of utter desolation. She didn't want to be left alone now. Spurned. It was important that he understand her reasons.

'Paul! Don't go!' she called, but the plaintive utterance was sliced in half by the slamming of the door.

Abject, lonely, Cassie abandoned herself to weeping.

'Did you have a good weekend?' asked Bridie chirpily as Cassie walked into the office on Monday morning.

'Fine, thanks. You?' Cassie went straight to her desk and set down her briefcase. 'Any coffee going, Lorraine?'

'Sure. I was just waiting for you to arrive.'

'Well, if you'd be an angel and rustle some up, we need to have a quick meeting. There are to be some changes. The section's coming down in size.'

'Coming down?' Bridie asked, indignant. 'But——'

'I know.' Cassie held up one hand to silence her. 'It's a real pain, I agree. And I'm absolutely livid about it. But I've decided we'll make the most of this opportunity to improve our act, to tighten up the editorial content. We're going to have more hard-hitting features, less froth.'

'But Penny Dreadful——' Bridie tried to interject, and she took off her spectacles and polished them on her plaid tunic.

'Penny Dreadful is dead.' Cassie drew one finger across her throat dramatically. 'She has been des-patched. She is no more. Anthony Holt has decided.'

'Ant said that?'

'Exactly, yes. Thanks, Lorraine.' For her secretary was handing her a steamy mug of Nescafé.

'Why would he do a thing like that? Oh, ta. Coffee. I need this.'

'Because, in his infinite wisdom, he thinks it will no longer have a place in the paper. There's to be a new section at the front of the Review: The Paul Roth Profile. And I'm afraid it's Roth we have to thank for the changes.'

'Paul Roth? Are you sure?' Bridie seemed surprised.

'Oh, quite sure. And, from what I hear, it's in character. John Stirling told me on Friday that Roth was pushy and arrogant.'

'He's dynamic, I'll give you that,' Bridie allowed, 'but I can't believe that he's behind this. It's not his style.'

'You'd better start believing it,' Cassie told her tersely, and she did not miss the quizzical look which Bridie shot her, as much as to ask, 'What's got into *you*?'

What had got into Cassie Murray was new resolve. Renewed determination. In a moment—or moments—of weakness, she had allowed her guard to come down. She'd let the mask slip. God, she had been on the point of succumbing to the sexuality of a colleague! It would have been a disaster, professional suicide, but fortunately she'd come to her senses in time.

Now she would work doubly hard at playing down her femininity. She would model herself on Bridie, whose solid good sense in life and in dress discouraged all male advances.

'I saw Paul Roth,' put in Lorraine dreamily. 'At least, I think it was him. He's the tall one, isn't he? I recognised him from his photograph. He was talking to Garry Schwarz by the noticeboard. He's dead good-looking. And he winked at me.'

Yes, Cassie told herself, that would be Roth's style. Giving a pretty girl the eye, tipping her the wink. That man had the morals of a goat! Fortunately, Lorraine, for all that she played the dizzy blonde, had her head firmly screwed on. She'd have a ring on her finger before she'd think of letting anyone share her bed.

What Cassie could not confront—could not admit to herself—was that the thought of Paul Roth making amorous advances to her secretary, or to any other woman, filled her with a sense of wretchedness and unutterable desolation.

She chose to perceive herself in the role of older sister, keeping a concerned eye on the younger girl. She would not own that jealousy was at work within her—or that it might tear her apart. She was not about to recognise the awful truth—that she had once again, aberrantly, foolishly, fallen in love.

'Lorraine, can you pop along to the art room?' she said briskly. 'Bring us half a dozen lay-out sheets. Then I'll sketch my ideas out and we can talk them through.'

When Lorraine had left the room, Bridie told Cassie, 'I can see how upset you are. And it really isn't fair. I'm sorry about your column, and I think it's madness.'

'That's all right,' Cassie told her. 'I can take it. I'm not going to let it get me down. The *In Touch* pages are going to be better than ever, I'm determined on it. We'll show 'em, eh?'

'Yes,' agreed Bridie, 'that we will.'

Working in isolation could be very productive—Cassie had spent most of Saturday and all of Sunday closeted in her flat, rethinking the editorial content of her section. But it was a relief, after so long, to have someone with whom to talk things through, someone who could act as a sounding board for her ideas. And, as ever, Bridie—never mind that she was not the most creative person—proved faultless in her judgment. At thirty-five, and with years of experience of the business of newspaper production, she was confident and sure-footed, and she gave generously of her expertise. Not for the first time, Cassie wondered how she would ever manage without her.

When, at half past one, Bridie announced, 'I'm dying of hunger, my stomach thinks my throat's cut, can we break for lunch?', Cassie would not have dreamed of demurring, although they had a few knotty problems still to unravel. 'I'm going to the canteen,' Bridie said. 'Will you keep me company?'

The staff canteen was a standing joke among the workers at the *Monitor*, for the tastelessness of both the décor and the fare. Convenience foods were served

without ceremony at a long display counter and
consumed from paper plates in the bleak expanse of
plastic and Formica which was the dining-area—
consumed, indeed, at great speed, since nothing about
the place encouraged lunchers to linger over endless
cups of coffee.

Cassie was usually content to forgo lunch altogether.
When she was absorbed in her work she had no
appetite, and she preferred not to cloud her perception
with alcohol. But it would have been unfriendly in the
extreme to turn Bridie down. So, 'That'd be nice,' she
lied courageously, hoping that there would be something
at least halfway tolerable on the day's menu.

Bridie cheerfully admitted that she had no interest in
good food, that she could live happily ever after on
instant concoctions from can, freezer and packet, and
that she was one of the few people who actually *liked*
the canteen for its no-nonsense approach to the dishing
up of fuel for the body. It was subsidised, wasn't it?
Why pay restaurant prices when you could pop
downstairs and fill up for fifty pence?

Together they stepped into the lift—the very same
one that had broken down on Friday night. Cassie held
her breath as her friend pressed the button for
'Basement'. Held it, not because she expected something
to go wrong again with the mechanism, but because she
was afraid to take in any of the tobacco-tainted air,
which still carried more than a faint whiff of a memory
for her. She imagined it going up her nostrils, invisible,
like millions of microscopic spores, inducing some kind
of infection in her mind.

'Hold it,' someone shouted, and they piled in, a crush
of people, so she was forced into a corner, to stand
where Paul Roth had sat so little time ago, looking up
at her in that insolent way of his.

When she closed her eyes momentarily, she saw his
face quite clearly and had to blink rapidly to erase the
image.

'Will you be going to see Ant today?' asked Bridie as

they strolled down the short corridor signposted 'Staff Restaurant'.

'If he has time. I'll ask Barbara—at least, if we set our thinking straight on those last few points.'

Between them they had produced a 'dummy'—a mock-up of the pages as they might in future look, with suggestions for the sort of shorter, denser features which were apparently wanted. Without any conceit, Cassie anticipated the Editor's approval. After all, she had risen to the challenge which he had laid down with a slap of the hand. In fact, she was actually beginning to feel quite excited about the changes, her imagination running ahead of her down the weeks, to the sort of stories they might carry in the spring and through to summer. If her only worries had been professional ones—if she were not nursing deep within her a sense of utter failure as a woman and feelings of terrible rejection—she would have felt quite in control of her destiny.

'You might ask him for a rise while you're at it,' suggested Bridie, canny as ever. 'He'll be feeling bad about cutting back on you. You know what a guilt complex he has. If he can put a few extra quid your way, it will help to salve his conscience.'

'He gave me a bonus when we were given the extra page,' Cassie laughed ruefully. 'I don't think I can ask for another one now it has been taken away.' But she privately resolved that she *would* put in a bid for more money—not for herself but for Bridie, who was long overdue for a merit increase.

'Yes?' asked the assistant impatiently, and Cassie opted without any real thought, but in eeny-meeny-miney-mo fashion, for sausage and beans, which came swimming in tomato sauce, with a cup of tea from a pot that would have held about a gallon.

'Bangers and beans,' said Bridie, the connoisseur of fast food, approving Cassie's choice, and she led on to a table, bearing aloft her own beefburger and French fries.

Once they were seated, Bridie began to relate a story
about her Auntie Morag, who was ninety if she was a
day, and who lived alone in a stone cottage, without
benefit of modern plumbing or electric light, and with
only a goat, a rabbit and numberless chickens for
company.

'She's trying to cheer me up,' Cassie realised with a
pang. 'Trying to take my mind off my problems.' Did it
show through, then, the misery on the inside? She'd
been wearing her new resolve like shining armour, but
Bridie McKay, sharp as a razor, must have sensed that
all was not well—though she could not have known the
true cause of the turmoil within.

She could not have known about Paul Roth.

And all at once there he was, standing not ten feet
off, holding a cup of coffee, speaking to Garry Schwarz,
head and shoulders taller than the slightly stocky, bull-
necked sports writer.

Roth was wearing a shirt of faded denim, the
bleached-out hue of it suiting very well his tanned face
and the lightness of his eyes, which were neither green
nor blue, which were not even grey—or, rather, which
were all three by turns, changing with the light.

On the bureau in Cassie's father's study, there was a
paperweight which had that same iridescent quality—
which could be now green, now blue, if you moved it
around so the rays of the sun caught it from this angle
then that. As a child, she had been fascinated by the
ornament, had loved to pick it up, to feel it solid in her
hand. She was put in mind of it now, for an instant.
Reminded of the panic she had felt, the fear of being
caught, since the study had been out of bounds for little
girls, and her father's kind face would have clouded
with annoyance to find her there.

She had known she would run into Roth, of course.
Sooner or later. She wouldn't be able to avoid him for
ever. But, please God, not here! Not in this place of
unpleasant food smells and clinically bright lights, to
the background clatter of knives and forks. Not

hemmed in, as she was, by a table, with a plate in front
of her of burnt sausage, of beans swimming in
improbable red sauce. The high-necked Cossack-style
blouse she was wearing seemed suddenly too tight
about her throat. It became an effort to swallow.

Perhaps, she thought, he might not see her. They
were looking, he and Garry, over the heads of the
people seated round and about, perhaps hoping to find
a corner table and a bit of privacy.

Her hand was trembling so she did not dare to pick
up her cutlery or even to chance a sip of tea. The food
lay untouched in front of her.

'Bridie! How're you doing? How's every little thing?'

It was Garry who spotted them, greeting Bridie
cheerfully, leading the way right to where they sat.

'Hi, Garry. Things are fine. You?'

'Terrific! Mind if we join you?'

And Bridie, naturally enough, told him, 'No, please,
sit down.'

'*He'll* feel as uncomfortable as I do,' Cassie
persuaded herself in desperation, her palms clammy, the
back of her neck prickling, her heart quickening
painfully. One hand, of its own volition rather than at
her behest, went beetling up to her throat to finger the
constricting collar. 'He'll be feeling every bit as
embarrassed as I do.'

But Paul Roth did not look the slightest bit ill at
ease. He sat down, nodded to them, even managed a
perfectly equable 'How do you do' when Garry, in his
innocence, introduced him to Cassie. Even managed a
smile for her—though there was nothing cosy or
friendly or forgiving about it, rather it was the
expression of someone enjoying a private joke,
indulging in some kind of ironic reflection. Cold, those
eyes were then, and curiously devoid of colour, beneath
the heavy brow.

'He knows me,' Cassie told herself, the full horror
dawning on her only now. 'He has known me in a way
that no man should. Especially no man who is my

colleague. He has . . . seen me. Heard me. He has—oh, my God!—*felt* me. Felt my very heartbeat. We have been that close. That close to making love. And now he's angry because he believes I led him on. That I set him up. He believes that I have taken my revenge in that way—that I'm the sort of girl who . . .'

'In fact, Cassie and I *have* met.'

He was speaking to Garry, although his eyes were trained on her like rifle sights, making her a target to be shot at. To be shot down.

For an unreasoning instant she imagined he was going to tell them everything that had happened on Friday night and on Saturday morning, drawing Bridie and Garry into the joke so they might all have a laugh at her expense.

'We had a meeting with Anthony on Friday evening. Rather unfortunate. He's cutting back on space for *In Touch*. I'm afraid Miss Murray has the idea that it was my doing.'

'No, she doesn't. She doesn't think that at all!' Bridie, staunch, rose automatically to take Cassie's part, while Cassie herself sat mute, framing her own reply in her head: 'You're damn right I have that idea! You just bet-ya I do!' There was, anyway, no need to voice that sentiment when her eyes, flashing fire, could say it so much more eloquently for her as she matched him, glare for glare.

'Ah-hem.' Garry Schwarz cleared his throat. 'I didn't realise there was any . . . er, needle between you. I'm sorry.'

'Oh, just a minor misunderstanding,' Paul assured him smoothly. 'Nothing, I'm sure, that we can't sort out.' With his now-familiar audacity, he seemed to be undressing her with his eyes, stripping off not merely her clothes—the high-necked silk shirt, under which, he would know, she was naked—but whole layers of her person, searching, probing, for the innermost her.

Cassie had a vision of those Russian dolls made of wood, with bland, smiling, painted faces, which come apart to reveal a smaller, though identical, doll within. And a smaller one and a smaller one ... With satisfaction she determined that he should look in vain for her secret being. Paul Roth would find it a thankless endeavour to take her apart. In each new layer he would find the same bland, smiling face, and the enigma would remain intact.

'Don't you want that sausage, honey?' Roth asked. 'Pity to waste it.' And, with flagrant cheek, he swiped it from her plate and took a bite.

Cassie said 'Russian dolls' to herself and repaid him with a smile. 'Have the beans as well if you like,' she invited, shoving the plate in his direction.

'No, you eat them. They're good for you. They're full of protein, you know. You could live on them.'

'I'd rather not, thanks, and I don't suffer from protein deficiency.'

'I never said you were deficient in anything,' he assured her, so that she burned with fear at what he might come out with next. 'I should say you were pretty *ee*-fficient. Pretty *su*-fficient. I should say you were pretty well all there. That's what I would say.'

'How very gratifying.'

'Sure.' He demolished the sausage and took a swig of his coffee.

'I'm just trying to recruit Paul for the *Monitor's* first eleven,' Garry said, clearly uncomfortable, discountenanced in the presence of so much hostility, trying to set the conversation back on a safe road for everyone's sake.

'Weren't you in it before?' Bridie asked Paul, valiantly joining the struggle to regain control of the situation.

'He was our star player before he went to New York. The best striker we ever had. The soccer team was top of the League,' Garry supplied.

'Then you *must* join again,' urged Bridie. 'Play for the newspaper.'

'We're counting on him.'

Paul Roth said neither yea nor nay, but kept his eyes focused on Cassie.

For her part, she saw it clearly. Saw *him* clearly. Pictured Roth in football gear, in the white shorts and blue shirt of the *Monitor* team. With what clarity she visualised muscular legs, deep-grooved behind the knees; a broad chest; the slightly over-long hair clinging to his intelligent brow. She could almost feel the damp warmth of his lightly perspiring body, to which the mud of the playing field would attach itself. She could almost hear the quickened breath, feel his accelerated heart-beat, smell the sweet moisture of his flesh.

He had, she told herself, that thing called 'animal magnetism'. It appealed not to the intellect, but to primitive instincts. Happily, *she* was not a primitive but a creature or intellect. 'I should think you would enjoy that,' she told him cuttingly. 'The *Roy of the Rovers* bit and all the glory-glory.'

'I quite enjoy the game, yes.'

'I mean, it's frightfully macho, isn't it? The thwack of boot against shin. A chance to chuck your weight about. And all those lovely heaving scrums.'

'They have scrums in Rugby, know-nothing, not in soccer.'

'But it's all somehow very scrummy. A game for *real* men.'

'I doubt you'd know a real man if you fell over him.'

Garry cut in, scolding them. 'Behave yourselves, you two, or I'll knock your heads together.'

Cassie saw in an instant that they were being disgracefully juvenile. 'If you'll excuse me,' she said, 'I have work to do.' And she stood up with all the hauteur she could muster and set off for the exit, knowing without a backward glance that Bridie was following, bemused but unquestioningly loyal.

Loyalty, however, did not demand that Bridie endorse such strange behaviour. Unspoken criticism accompanied them on their journey to the fourth floor and their dreary workplace, where the colourful festoons seemed almost to point up the grime.

'Go on, say it,' Cassie told her with a sigh when she closed the office door and crossed to her desk. 'I suppose you think I made an exhibition of myself back there.'

'An exhibition? Not exactly.' Bridie removed her spectacles and polished them on her tartan skirt, then held them to the window to inspect the lenses. 'In fact, rather the opposite. I felt I was eavesdropping on something intensely private.'

'I'm sorry.'

'I don't know why you have it in for Paul in such a way. I've known him for a long time, Cassie, and I think a lot of him. There aren't many like him. Not with his talent and his integrity.'

'I can only say,' Cassie replied coolly, 'that I must have seen a side to Paul Roth that hasn't been apparent to you.'

'Stubborn, you,' said Bridie, who was no respecter of rank when it came to speaking her mind. 'Him as well. Perhaps that's the problem. Yes, that could be it.'

'Maybe you're right.' Cassie was suddenly business-like. She did not care to discuss the matter further. 'Anyway, shall we get on? Agree to differ? You're entitled to your view, after all, as I am to mine.'

'Indeed,' said Bridie, who had an extraordinary knack, as Cassie had noticed before, of making one word do the work of a dozen, as though Scottish thrift could be brought to bear on the language with the same effect as on the household budget. Verbally, that girl could make a little go a very, very long way.

'I think it's going to snow again.' Lorraine came in at that moment with pretty, pink cheeks and this depressing prognosis. And, sure enough, beyond the windows, the sky had taken on that peculiar, dirty yellow tinge which can portend a blizzard.

'My giddy aunt,' murmured Bridie, 'that's all we need!'

'Oh, I think it would be lovely!' Lorraine told them. 'So romantic! A white Christmas, like in all the pictures.'

'Brr, you can keep it. Nasty, slippery stuff. It's all right for you, but in Argyll where I come from, you see too much snow to think it's anything but a nuisance.'

'What are you two going to wear to the office party?' Lorraine then wanted to know.

'I shall go as I am,' Bridie informed her. 'I always do. I can't see the point in changing, getting all done up like a Christmas tree.'

'Oh.' Lorraine looked crestfallen.

'I thought I might skip it altogether,' Cassie confided. 'I must say, I'm not in the party mood.'

Lorraine's face fell a little further.

'But a lot of the girls will be dressing up,' Bridie assured the young secretary kindly. 'There's nothing to stop you if you want to.'

'Well,' Lorraine, brightening, set a carrier-bag on the desk, 'I've been down Oxford Street. Bought myself a little number. Would you like to see it?'

'Oh, yes, do show us!' Cassie urged her, not wanting to be a wet blanket. If Christmas was still a magical time for Lorraine, then good luck to her! It was enviable, really, being able to look forward to it with such wide-eyed, wholehearted wonder.

From the folds of tissue paper, Lorraine produced an evening-dress with beaded bodice and flouncing skirts, layer upon layer of rustling taffeta, black with silver piping, a dress very much in the spirit of Christmas and of fun.

'That's fantastic!' Cassie told her as Lorraine held it against herself and performed a little twirl on tiptoe. 'You'll be the belle of the ball.'

'So long as some of the others really will get done up,' Lorraine sought further reassurance. 'I mean, it wouldn't do for me to be the only one looking like a fairy on a rock cake.'

'Well, I've not been to a Christmas party here before.' Cassie reminded her. 'Like you, I only joined the staff this year.'

'You'll be all right,' Bridie insisted. 'You'll be in good company.'

'Like I say,' Cassie mused, 'I may actually give it a miss this year anyway.'

'You'll do no such thing!' Bridie scolded. 'What can you be thinking of? You have a duty to show your face. There'll be freelance contributors coming as our guests, and you'll be their hostess. It would be terribly bad form to duck out.'

'I suppose so,' Cassie agreed, seeing the truth in this. She had appended to the guest-list being circulated to department heads the names of a number of writers and illustrators who had worked for *In Touch* in her time there. Their invitations would have been issued as from her personally as editor of the section.

'I mean, I'd feel a real wally,' Lorraine persisted.

'For the last time,' Bridie sighed, 'there'll be lots of the girls dressing up. Most of them. It's only the old stick-in-the-muds like Cassie and me who won't be donning our best bibs and tuckers.'

A memo had fallen from the noticeboard. Cassie went to retrieve it, driving the drawing-pin in with her thumb. 'Old stick-in-the-mud'? Was this the light in which other people saw her? A frump, no less. Asked to describe herself, she would have played with words like 'aloof', 'contained', even 'unattainable'. But not—oh, no, never!—'old stick-in-the-mud'. 'Thus we see ourselves,' she thought. 'Through the little chinks in conversation. So we are afforded glimpses of the person others see. And the rest is mere delusion.'

'*You* could wear a dress like this,' Lorraine addressed herself to Cassie's back. 'I reckon it'd look amazing.'

'Not my style,' Cassie replied tersely, and she turned to give a wan smile. 'How about some coffee, Lorraine? Then there are some cuttings to photo-copy. We must get on, Bridie and I.'

Lorraine did not immediately respond. She held the dress at arms' length, considering. 'Maybe I'll get myself a fellah at the party.'

'I should think you'll get yourself a dozen,' Cassie told her wryly. 'You'll be fighting them off.'

'Oh, I don't mean some old groper from the business pages, or one of those louts of messengers. I mean someone really nice and dishy and eligible. Someone like Paul Roth.'

'*Coffee*, please, Lorraine.'

'Oh, sorry. I'll hang it up in the fashion cupboard, shall I? Get changed in the office when the time comes. There's no sense in taking it all the way home, only to bring it back here.'

'Yes, do that,' Cassie agreed, shuffling papers, feeling a mite school-ma'amish. What an old maid she might grow to be, given time! Perhaps she ought to rethink her whole act—but not now. For there really was work to do. 'And when you've done the photo-copying, can you give Barbara a buzz? Ask if the Editor has any time to see me this afternoon. There's a love.'

'Sure,' said Lorraine cheerfully, cramming the billowing skirts into the metal lock-up cupboard. 'You're the boss.' And, more to herself than to Cassie, 'I still reckon you'd knock 'em dead if you'd only take a bit of extra trouble over your appearance.'

As she had predicted, Cassie was afforded a pat on the back by Anthony Holt, whom she found at his most paternalistic this afternoon. 'Well done, well done,' he commended her as he perused the dummy page lay-outs. 'Didn't I say you could do it?'

'You did say.' She repaid him with only the merest smile, for she was still angry at the way she'd been treated and did not intend to let him know that she felt gratified by his approval. 'While I'm here, I'd like to talk to you about Bridie McKay.'

How shrewd Bridie was! How astute! Cassie reflected on this as she returned to the *In Touch* office, the meeting with Anthony successfully concluded. There could not have been a better time to mention the matter of money to him. Bridie would be pleased when he called her in tomorrow and, with the beneficence of Father Christmas himself, informed her that she was going to get a rise.

The office was by now deserted. Bridie and Lorraine had gone home—though not before Lorraine, as was her custom, had put the covers on all their typewriters, 'putting them to bed' as she called it.

Cassie went to her own desk and slid the pages, which now bore Anthony's signature, his endorsement, into the top drawer. A set of keys lay in the pen trays—for the door to the room, for the filing-cabinets, for the fashion cupboard, where samples from the designers were kept ready for photography.

When Cassie glanced up she was confronted by her own reflection, pale and spectral, in the inky blue glass of the window.

'Old stick-in-the-mud'?

On a sudden impulse, she grabbed up the keys and went to lock the office door from the inside. Then, with her heart all a-flutter, she went and opened the fashion cupboard.

The dress hung there still. Lorraine's dress.

'You'd knock 'em dead if you'd only take a little trouble.'

Lorraine didn't properly understand. She didn't realise that Cassie in fact *did* take trouble, went to no end of effort over her appearance.

Cassie Murray went through life in disguise.

With fumbling fingers, she unbuttoned the blouse which had earlier seemed so constricting, let it float over a chair. She kicked off her boots and scrambled out of her slacks to stand there, shivering slightly, in just her pants and tights.

Swish went the dress, over her head, and how snugly it fitted her when she reached behind to close the zip! With her two hands she pulled her hair up above her head, then let it fall about her face.

The woman who confronted her from the mirror-glass of the window now was a new Cassie Murray.

And, yes, she would have knocked 'em dead.

CHAPTER FOUR

WITH a hiss and rattle the tube train issued from the blackness of the tunnel and drew to a halt beside the sweep of platform, where people jostled each other in their anxiety to get aboard. Inside the carriages, other travellers jostled with equal anxiety to get out. In the instant before the doors parted, Cassie was struck by their likeness to marine creatures in a zoo, viewed through an observation window.

What a strange, twilight world this was beneath the streets of the capital! Cassie preferred to take the bus, to be in daylight. But this morning, unusually, her alarm had failed to penetrate her slumbers. Perhaps the emotional highs and lows of the past few days—and Friday seemed like an eternity ago—had overtired her, for she wasn't very strong. Anyway, she'd woken late and had decided to go by underground ('the subway', Paul Roth had called it), since it would be quicker. She found herself packed between businessmen in suits, in one of the central aisles, hanging on to a strap for grim death as the train clattered round the bends.

'Nightmare, isn't it?' said a voice, and looking down she saw Barbara Drew, Anthony Holt's secretary, sitting there with some crochet on her lap, the hook flying as she deftly worked a scarf in yellow wool. 'Christmas present,' she explained in answer to Cassie's unspoken question. 'For my old gran.'

At Camden Town, the man in the seat next to Barbara folded his paper, tucked it under his arm and stood up. 'Phew!' said Cassie, thankfully, sitting down.

'Doing anything for Christmas?' Barbara wanted to know.

'Oh, I shall go and see my parents. They live in Hampshire. They would be upset if I didn't visit.'

'You an only child?'

'Yes.'

'I have four brothers. All older than me. Where are we?'

'Coming up to Euston,' Cassie told her as they eased into the station. 'With a bit of luck, people will start getting off.'

They journeyed on in silence to Leicester Square, Barbara frowning over her pattern, scratching her head with the crochet hook through her knitted, teacosy hat. Then she said, 'I'm sorry about your column.'

'My . . .?'

'Penny Dreadful. I'm sorry it's been given the chop. It was one of the best things on a Sunday morning. I always used to turn straight to it.'

'It's kind of you to say so.'

'I speak as I find. I think it's a pity, but there it is. Once Anthony decides . . .' Barbara's fingers resumed their nimble working of the wool.

'I'm not sure that it was Anthony's idea,' Cassie confided grimly, thinking of Roth.

'No?' asked Barbara, jabbing the hook into the ball of wool and cramming the lot into a John Lewis carrier-bag. 'How comes that, then?'

'What? Oh, *that*. Well, I think . . .' said Cassie as they stood up to change at Embankment station, 'it was Paul Roth suggested it—made it a condition of coming back to be *Prud'homme*.'

The tiled subterranean passageway rang with their footsteps, which seemed to run ahead of them, to lie in wait for them around the corner. As the escalator bore them upwards to the next level, Barbara informed her, 'You're wrong, you know.'

'I'm sorry?'

Barbara did not volunteer any further information, though Cassie could tell she was mulling something over. As personal secretary to the Editor, Barbara Drew was in a position of trust which called for absolute discretion. She had always honoured this, and Cassie knew it would be unfair to try to quiz her. Not only that, but it would be futile: Barbara was not the type to respond to cross-questioning. All the same, Cassie burned to know more.

A train came and they stepped aboard. Barbara looked to right and left, saw that there was no one to overhear, and seemed to take a decision. 'There was a memo,' she said in a conspiratorial undertone. 'This was before Nick Moy left. Saying the women's coverage would be cut back. It was suggested that there should be a major personality profile by one of our top-flight reporters—probably Nick—and Penny Dreadful would go. Anthony dictated the memo and I typed it, but if you ask me it was the editorial directors' idea. You know what old fogeys they are, and Anthony can't always be standing up to them, he has to save himself for the really important fights. Anyway, in the middle of all this, Nick and Anthony had a row and Nick walked out.'

'And Paul Roth walked in?'

'Precisely.'

They said not another word as they mounted the steps to the barrier and found their way into the street. The threatened snow had not materialised; the day was grey and dry.

'I'm telling you this,' said Barbara, 'because you should know the truth. You shouldn't go laying blame at the wrong door.'

'I understand,' said Cassie, sensing that Barbara was already regretting her very minor indiscretion, for she gnawed her nether lip and looked miserable as they approached the office. 'But of course, it's all strictly between ourselves.'

'In fact, Paul Roth was singing your praises,' Barbara revealed. She had a way of imparting information erratically, in great dollops. Cassie waited, hoping there would be yet more—and there was. 'I was putting the coffee on, you see. And Anthony was outlining his plans to Paul while they were waiting for you to arrive, and Paul was raising all kinds of queries. He said he thought you had exceptional talent. He said it would be a shame to axe your column—a shame for the paper and a shame for you, since it might discourage you. He said someone as promising as you should be nurtured—his exact words.'

Cassie felt a curious warm sensation, a glow in her chest, around the area of her heart. Gratitude seemed to radiate through her—to Barbara for breaking all her professional rules in the interests of fairness, and to Paul for so gallantly taking her part.

'Quite a spirited defence he put up for you,' Barbara said. And, summing up her dilemma, 'I wish I hadn't told you—though I'm glad I did.'

'I promise you . . .' Cassie crossed her heart superstitiously with one finger. 'My lips are sealed.'

'It's not that I don't trust you, only . . .'

'I know how you feel.' Cassie reached out and gave Barbara's arm a friendly squeeze. She would have been about thirty-eight or nine, and she was the sort of woman whom people will describe as 'salt of the earth'. Cassie doubted if Barbara Drew had a mean bone in her body.

'What are you two gossiping about?' asked Peter Playfair, education correspondent, joining them in the lobby.

'About the office party tomorrow night,' Cassie lied bare-facedly.

'Ah, yes.' He rubbed his hands together; they made the sound of parchment. 'Should be a good do. You'll be there, won't you, Cassie?'

'You bet,' she said with feigned enthusiasm. If she had to put in an appearance, she decided, she might as well do so with a good grace.

There was a lightness in her now, a lightness of heart. She had been wrong about Paul Roth, she had misjudged him. Headstrong as ever, she had refused to listen to those who knew better—to people like Bridie who had assured her that meanness was not Roth's style.

But the sense of emotional weightlessness was short lived. Almost at once it gave way to other, more complex emotions.

First to knock on the door of her conscience came Guilt, demanding to be admitted. She should be ashamed of herself, she realised, for being so ready to think ill of someone, in spite of the counsel of others who knew better.

Hard on the heels of Guilt came Doubt. Self-doubt. Because if she could so badly misjudge a situation, how wrong might she have been many times in the past?

Then Anger was back with her as she reminded herself that Paul Roth, while he might have been cleared of one charge, still stood accused of being a seducer.

Cassie's thinking was never wholly straightforward. That she could pen sweet, succinct, well-reasoned paragraphs was somewhat misleading—for no one but she could know the mental excursions on which she must go before arriving at a single conclusion. She had the kind of labyrinthine mind in which ideas might wander endlessly, taking all manner of twists and turns in search of a solitary truth.

Now she began to wonder why Roth had not tried harder to convince her that the proposed changes—the axing of her column, the cutting back of her section— were not his doing.

'You're wrong,' he'd said, or something of the sort. But in so mild, so unpersuasive a way!

Perhaps he had been laughing at the spectacle of her rage, allowing her to make an idiot of herself, to be foolish in his eyes. Worst of all, he might have encouraged her anger, believing that the energy it generated might be converted into sexuality, of which he could take full advantage.

By the time she arrived at her desk, Cassie's head was spinning with so much speculation.

'How are you today?' Bridie greeted her. 'When you've settled in, can you call Fiona in the production department? And Liz Anderson phoned to say she was never paid for the interview with the battered wives lady.'

'I'll chase up the invoice,' Cassie promised, picking up the phone, running her pencil down the list on the wall in search of Fiona's number.

'It's 4282,' supplied Bridie the mind-reader. 'I've sorted the morning's post, it's all here. Forward planning meeting this afternoon, four o'clock, Editor's office. I've put it in your diary.'

'All right.' It was faintly irksome to Cassie, the way Anthony Holt always referred to 'forward planning'. In her book, this was the only kind of planning possible. If only it were not so! If only you could plan your past as well! With the benefit of hindsight, if we could rearrange what had gone before, such tidy little lives we would lead.

It had preoccupied her through many a sleepless night, the longing to be able to rework whole passages, if not whole chapters, of her own story. Gwyn, whom she had loved so much, and that entire episode of heartbreak, would then have no place in the narrative. And she would have handled so much better, those intense—and intensely embarrassing—interludes with Paul Roth . . .

It was beginning to seem that she had only to think his name—had only to articulate it to herself—for him to materialise before her eyes. At that very moment, he walked through the door and came right over, cool as you please, half smiling, slightly sardonic.

'Hi,' Cassie acknowledged him, though she kept him waiting while she hung on for Fiona to pick up her extension and then discussed with her some changes to the printing schedule.

Not the least discountenanced, Roth dragged a chair over, straddled it, and amused himself by making a necklace of paperclips which he scooped in one big handful from her pen tray. It was an act of studied nonchalance which somehow made her own little power ploy seem infantile and faintly pathetic.

When she replaced the receiver, he, in his turn, said 'Hi'. He was wearing a check shirt, unbuttoned to the little hollow of his chest. His hair had the softness which very recent washing imparts. His eyes, this morning, were distinctly green. No, greeny-blue. Well, really more blue than green. As he allowed the loose paperclips to dribble from his bunched fist on to the desk top, she noticed a fine golden down at his wrist, and thought how strong those hands would be. She could imagine him arm-wrestling in a bar, his mouth set in a taut line as he pitted his strength against another's. An absurd scenario, of course, for he was a man of greater refinement.

'Sorry about that.'

'Don't worry. I understand. You're a busy woman.' He rocked on the chair. She thought it must be the shirt that lent him the air of a cowboy.

She wanted to say, 'Look, I hope we're not going to conduct all our conversations, ever after, in this sarcastic vein. It really could get very tiresome.' Instead she heard herself enquire, not without a certain starchiness, 'What can I do for you?'

'We ought to have that lunch.'

'What lunch?' She remembered now that he had suggested it, on Friday, at their first meeting. Suggested that they might take the opportunity to get 'properly acquainted'.

'I thought we had a date for this week,' he said smoothly.

'When did you have in mind, exactly?'

'Today.'

'I'm ... not sure. I don't know if I can.'

With his long arm he reached across to snatch up her desk diary. 'You're not sure if you're free? Let's have a look, shall we?'

'I've nothing booked in.' She snatched the diary away from him indignantly, feeling splashes of colour on her pale cheeks. 'It's just that I was hoping to do some Christmas shopping.'

'Can't it wait? Christmas is a long way off yet.'

'A week, to be precise. Six shopping days.'

'That's what I mean. Ages.'

Half of her wanted to say yes; the other half cautioned against it. In the expectant silence the click of the latch as Bridie left the room sounded loud in their ears.

For a moment, they were alone. At once he leaned forward and placed his hand over hers, covering it. 'Cassie,' he said softly, softly, in a voice that reached right into her and found kind response, 'don't be hard on me. I'm sorry about what happened—about Friday night, about coming on so strong. I shouldn't have blamed you, it wasn't your fault. I know I overstepped the mark. But I so wanted . . . Now I just want us to be friends.'

She had thought of him as her rival, her enemy. For a few breathless moments she might have entertained him as her lover. But . . . friends?

'Pax.' He made the schoolboy sign with his fingers, appealingly. And then added, *'Please.'*

There were two Cassie Murrays. One of them was soft and pliable, infinitely forgiving, wanting now— aching and longing—to get up and twine her arms about this man's neck, to touch her lips to his cheek and feel the roughness of the morning's growth of beard. The other Cassie, the dominant one, was confused and angry and still bitter against all men, sitting rigid, unable or unwilling to move one inch towards him.

'Sorry I'm late,' said Lorraine, coming flustered into the office at the psychological moment.

'That's all right,' Cassie told her, coming to a hurried compromise inside herself. And, 'All right then, today will be fine . . . er, Paul.'

'It's a date, then.' He stood up, smiling. 'About one o'clock? I'll come by for you, shall I?'

Turning his attentions to Lorraine, he asked, 'Have I taken your chair? I'm sorry. Here.'

'That's all right,' Lorraine assured him, blushing, giggling, as he returned the chair to its rightful place.

Cassie felt herself obscurely annoyed. 'I want you to do some letters,' she said quite brusquely to her secretary as the door closed behind Roth.

'Of course.' Lorraine looked crestfallen: she was unused to being spoken to in this way.

'Sorry, I didn't mean this instant. When you're ready.' Cassie tried to cover herself, to cover up. It occurred to her that she might be, in her way, every bit as obvious as Lorraine. A blush could tell a tale—but so could a hardness about the eyes or in the voice, a blenched lip or a grim mouth.

She was also profoundly shocked by the 'Hands off!' reaction which had been sparked in her, a white-hot flash of jealousy and possessiveness. Heaven knows, Paul Roth was nothing to her. At best they might hope for the friendship he claimed to be looking for. He was not her property, or anyone else's—rather, rumour had it, he was common property, there for the taking by any good-looking young woman who was so minded. If Lorraine felt attracted to him then good luck to her, though Cassie would not give much for her chances of more than a casual fling with him.

'He's ever so handsome, isn't he?' Lorraine sighed.

'Who? Oh, Roth. Yes, I suppose so.' Cassie had a grip on herself once more. 'Sorry if I sounded snappy just then. It's only that I've been working rather hard lately.'

'I understand,' said Lorraine, who, of course, didn't really understand at all.

'Mirror, mirror, on the wall . . .' Cassie engaged herself—engaged her looking-glass image—for a lingering moment in contemplation of her personal charms. But the trick was, of course, to look quickly—to glance and turn immediately away. To catch yourself unawares. Gaze into your own eyes and you see only distortion; your features seem to wax and wane.

In any case, it was too unprivate, the office cloakroom, with people barging in and out. It was no place for self-assessment beyond the daily routine check-up. Hair, all right. Make-up, passable.

She had on a flame-coloured blouse with her tailored, navy blue jacket and skirt. All these clothes she had bought by mail-order through offers in fashion magazines. It suited her well to shop this way: it was convenient, it saved wear and tear on the nerves and on shoe leather, and, being a neat size 10, there was never a problem over fit.

The blouse, however, had been a mistake. Theirs rather than hers. She'd sent for a white one, or thought she had. It was possible—but not very likely—that, in a distracted moment, she had ticked the wrong box for colour choice. Certainly she would not intentionally have opted for this very vivid shade of orange.

Her first reaction had been to send the offending garment back, but somehow she hadn't got around to it within the fourteen days' grace for return of goods. Then there had seemed no sense in leaving the stupid thing hanging around—so she'd tried it on.

It suited her. It set off her dark eyes, her velvety hair. It still wasn't *her* in the sense that it originated from quite another area of the colour spectrum from the one she had made her own. But she could not deny to herself that it looked more than merely all right on her. She'd paid for it, too, so why not wear it?

On impulse this morning, for the first time since the early, tentative trying-on session, she had taken it from its hanger in the wardrobe. She'd confirmed her earlier impression that the shade of it actually enhanced rather than sabotaged the subtle colouring of her cheeks. She had fastened at the throat a Victorian Cupid's-bow-and-heart brooch which had been her great-grand-mother's. And she'd passed herself fit for the day.

Now she found herself wondering if she'd have felt more at ease in her usual cream or white, whose neutrality would not impinge on her consciousness.

When she was feeling shy—and she somehow knew that shyness would attend this lunch with Roth—she preferred not to be too aware of herself in any physical sense.

'He's there. In the office. Waiting for you.' Lorraine came hurriedly through the door and disappeared into one of the cubicles.

'Who is?' asked Cassie innocently.

'Paul Roth of course. You've got a date, haven't you?'

'Not a date.' Cassie tucked her leather clutch-bag under her arm and braced herself, pushing her shoulders back. 'Nothing of the sort. Just a working lunch.'

She found Paul standing, as he had been at their first meeting, with his back to the room, peering through the window, down into the central well, or across the void to other offices to right, to left, or directly facing this one.

'Hello,' she said.

'Hi.' He turned and flashed her one of his biggest and best smiles. 'Are you ready? I thought we could go to the new Japanese restaurant if you liked. All the usual watering-holes will be full of drunks topping up with Christmas spirit. I'd sooner go somewhere less frenetic.'

'That's fine by me,' she assured him, not choosing to voice any doubts. She'd eaten Japanese food before and knew it wasn't all raw fish and sitting barefoot and cross-legged. Not here in London, anyway. But in a way, unusually for her, she might have preferred to go where the crowd was, where work-mates would see them and might even join them. Some craven part of her was very afraid of being alone with Roth—though she did not even try to think through her reasons for this.

'We'll take a cab,' he proposed as they stepped outside the building, 'it's too far to walk in this weather, and not far enough to drive. Not worth getting the car out—and not a cat's chance in hell of finding anywhere to park.'

'Whatever you prefer,' she agreed.'

At once he went windmilling out into the road to flag down a speeding taxi on the other side. Cassie was left stranded, like a reluctant swimmer, paddling there at the kerb, trying to pluck up courage to wade out after him into the sea of vehicles.

Paul glanced over his shoulder, laughed at her, and came back to fetch her, clasping her about the wrist and towing her in his wake. 'You wouldn't last five minutes in New York, you know.'

'I realise that,' she said, laughing too, as they bundled into the back of the cab. 'I've always been a nervous road-crosser.'

'The secret is not to hesitate. The minute you do, you're . . .'

'Lost.'

'Exactly.'

This was one of the few London black cabs which still had leather upholstery. The smell of it in the heated interior was deliciously luxurious. The fan positively roared out warm air.

'I like that blouse you're wearing,' Paul said.

Up went her hand, of its own volition, to finger the antique brooch at her throat. 'Do you? I'm not sure about it. It was a sort of . . . mistake.'

'It doesn't look like one. It looks great.'

'Well . . . thanks.'

She sat back in the seat and privately took herself to task. She was giving in to natural shyness, and that *simply wasn't good enough*. She must get a grip on herself this instant. Regain her composure. She'd learned the trick of it, after all, the art of appearing self-confident. She'd been playing the cool professional for all she was worth since she arrived at the *Monitor*, and everyone accepted her as such. None of her other colleagues—why, not even Anthony Holt—made her feel so unsure of herself as she did with Roth.

For his part, he made no attempt at small talk, but seemed content to lounge there, in that peculiarly

relaxed way of his, staring out at the streetscape, at the
lunchtime shoppers jostling each other off the pavements. Cassie read the advertisements on the undersides
of the fold-down seats and hoped that whatever had
struck her dumb would loose her tongue before too
long.

In the restaurant Paul Roth became instantly
conversational, expansive and utterly charming. It was
a beautiful place, as Cassie had expected, with hand-
painted paper screens through which light filtered
palely, gently. Most of the tables were occupied, the
staff were kept busy, but there was an air of calm, of
tranquillity, quite at odds with the push and shove, the
panic which had the rest of the city in its grip.

When the street door was opened and closed, wind
chimes tinkled musically, merrily, and the paper
lanterns bobbed.

'I thought we could sit through there at the bar,'
suggested Paul, 'and have *tempura* . . . if you liked.'

'That would be lovely,' Cassie assured him, for she
would be fascinated to watch the chef at his work—at
his art—deftly fashioning bite-size morsels of seafood
and vegetables, frying them in a batter as thin and
transparent as silken gauze. Thus they perched side by
side on stools at a counter, behind which a young
Japanese man, quite exquisite of feature, plied the tools
of his trade.

Cassie remembered now, sitting opposite Paul in the
intimacy of Pinello's restaurant. Remembered the press
of his knee against hers, which she had somehow
known was not accidental. And it occurred to her that
he had chosen this place quite deliberately because,
warm and friendly though it was, it lacked the dark and
steamy atmosphere in which desire might thrive.

His next words confirmed it. 'I'd like,' he said, 'if it's
possible, for us to begin again.'

'Begin . . .?' She raised an eyebrow in enquiry.

'You know. Pretend we've only just met. Ignore all
that's gone before.'

'All right,' she agreed, taking a sip of fragrant green tea.

'I mean, if we could ... not literally, of course, but figuratively speaking ... if we could pretend we'd just been introduced. Say "How do you do" and "Pleased to make your acquaintance".'

'How do you do,' said Cassie wryly. 'I'm pleased to make your acquaintance.'

'Then you think it's possible? To ... you know, return to "Go" and try and throw another six?'

The board-game image was all at once very vivid. Cassie saw in her mind's eye the long, arduous ladders and the mischievous, slippery snakes that must be negotiated in her relationship with this man. 'It's all right with me,' she smiled gently, ruefully.

'I'd like to do it ... if we're able.'

Able? Well, of course, one could always pretend. Make believe. *Anyone* could do that. But deep down there might be no denying the realities. No denying that they had been combatants. That they might have been lovers. That a tension pulled between them, this way, that way, even now, at this moment, though their behaviour was rational enough.

'After all, we both have a job to do.'

'That's right.'

'And we can't avoid each other. Not all the time. Not for ever.'

'Certainly we can't.'

'What we *can* do is to declare a truce.'

Two more reasonable, more amenable people, Cassie thought with private amusement, you could hardly wish to meet.

'Let's drink to it then,' Paul suggested. 'To friendship.' And, as she lifted her little cup of green tea, 'We should order some *sake*. That is, if you like it.'

'I *do*. Very much.'

'Just the thing in this cold weather.'

He summoned the waiter, who brought a lacquer tray of tiny beakers, different in shape—some bigger, some more rotund than others; some like very large thimbles—but each with a delicate hand-painted design. The warmed rice wine arrived in a blue and white jug and Paul poured a little for Cassie.

'To friendship, then,' she said, and he filled his own beaker and raised it to her. And it must have been the blue swirls of colour on the white china which made his eyes today appear so outrageously, innocently blue.

A curious taste, *sake* had, mused Cassie as the liquid blazed its way down her throat. She was rather cross with herself in one respect, for breaking her usual rule about alcohol—about drinking during the working day. She had managed to pull herself together; she knew— or, anyway, hoped—that she was outwardly poised. But inside she was still slightly trembly and unsure, and no glib talk of 'friendship' was going to alter *that*.

They addressed themselves hungrily to the offerings of the chef—to the delectable mouthfuls of clam and cuttlefish, baby scallops, shrimp and eel, to tiny whitebait and strips of sole, mushrooms, spring onions, prawns with chrysanthemum leaves and seaweed, slivers of fresh ginger, delicate slices of lotus root. No sooner had she eaten one thing than Cassie found another, still sizzling from the pan, in the bowl in front of her.

'In ancient times,' Roth informed her, 'the Japanese used to eat foods in a certain order: first the produce of the mountains, then the harvest of the ocean, then of the fields.' He plied his own chopsticks with alacrity and with a neatness unexpected of such large hands. Watching him, Cassie would not have been surprised to be told that he was also skilled at needlework—or could be if he put his mind to it, which she could not imagine him doing. No, he'd be too impatient to do more than sew on the occasional button. He'd have trouble threading the needle, would try to force it on to the cotton the way very masculine men always did, instead of guiding the cotton through the needle's eye.

'It makes our own way of eating seem rather prosaic, doesn't it?' she commented.

She wondered what he lived on at home alone—supposing he ever was alone. He might, for all she knew, pay someone to come in and cook for him. And the succession of bed-mates whom rumour attributed to him would no doubt fall over themselves to make his morning tea and toast. His evening meal, too, given half a chance.

'Can *you* cook, Cassie? Any good at it, are you?'

'*Can,*' she allowed, 'but don't. Not much. I mean, it's hardly worth it for oneself.' Catching the look of disapproval which he shot her, and anxious to head him off if he proposed to lecture her in the you-should-look-after-yourself vein, she hastened to explain, 'Oh, don't misunderstand me, I think nutrition is very important. And I hate junk food, badly-cooked food. It's such a criminal waste, somehow, of the world's resources. And such an insult. But I live quite simply. An omelette will usually do me, or cheese on toast. In any case, who feels like cooking after a day's work?'

'I do,' he told her. 'I like to cook. It's fun, it's creative and it's actually a good way of relaxing. I'm not saying I'm good at it—only that I enjoy it. On the other hand, I'm not half bad. You must come to supper one night and see what I can do.'

'I'd like that,' she said politely, for there was no hint of innuendo, not a breath of suggestiveness about the invitation. Genuinely, then, he was sorry for over-stepping the mark with her. Genuinely, he wanted to make amends.

'Though of course, in our line of work, one finds one's out most evenings,' he said, sipping his rice wine.

'Yes, one does,' she lied.

He talked on, then, about this and that—opera, ballet, theatre . . . No wonder, she thought, he had been chosen to take over *Prud'homme*. There was certainly no one working on the paper with wider interests or breadth of education.

Remembering what Barbara had told her that morning, it occurred to Cassie now that, in some

respects at least, she owed this man an apology. But
how to tell him she was sorry, without explaining what
had changed her mind? 'Paul . . .' she began, embarrassed.

'Yes?'

'Look, the other evening. After our meeting with
Anthony. I jumped to a few conclusions. To the *wrong*
conclusions, as it now seems.'

'Never mind about that now. It's all forgotten, isn't
it? Didn't we agree? Like we only just met. None of it
happened.'

'I know all that.' She flapped her hands around in
mild irritation. 'But it *did* happen, and I should like to
apologise.'

'Accepted,' he told her dismissively.

'Just one question: *why* didn't you put me straight?'

'I did. I told you you were wrong.'

'Not very persuasively. You couldn't have expected
me to believe . . . I mean, you really just let it go. You
hardly protested your innocence at all.'

'Would you have believed me if I did?'

'Probably not,' she confessed, and the laugh she
uttered was against herself and her own intransigence.

'Anyway,' he teased, 'you're lovely when you're
angry.'

Both of them realised in an instant that the
conversation had somehow strayed off limits. An
embarrassed silence settled on them, which was broken
only when he asked, in conversational tone, 'Are you
going to the office party tomorrow night, then?'

'I'm told I have to.' Cassie smiled as she remembered
Bridie's stern rebuke. 'Mistress McKay informs me that
it's my duty to be there and play hostess to our
freelance contributors. She has a point, of course.'

'She does. She's absolutely right. But even if she
weren't, don't you think you might enjoy it? It's
traditionally quite a good night, you know. Everyone
has a good time. I was disappointed to miss it myself,
last year, being in the States and everything.'

'I don't know . . .' Cassie toyed with her chopsticks as she reflected. 'I'm not much of a partygoer. I used to be when I was younger——'

'But now, at your advanced age . . . How old *are* you, by the way?'

She gave him one of her most reproving looks.

His reaction, then, was to chuckle delightedly. 'Sorry, sorry, I know one's not supposed to ask. But if you don't tell me, I shall simply look up the old cuttings. About the Margaret Thingummy Award. I can always find these things out by stealth if I want to, though I prefer to be open and direct.'

'No, find out the hard way. Why should I make it easy for you? Look up the cuttings if you must.' Cassie was laughing, too, because he was quite right. There was little that one journalist on the *Monitor* could not find out about another if he or she put his mind to it. She herself would not be above a little investigative work on the quiet to find out more about the person who had been, until this week, the New York correspondent.

He poured her more *sake*. 'You're a slip of a girl, at any rate, Miss Murray. And I'm glad you're going to be at the office party because I've promised myself a dance with you . . . to cement our new friendship,' he put in hastily, reading a warning in her eyes.

'I shall have to see if I can fit you in,' she teased.

They shared a smile, warm, amicable, understanding. All anger, all resentment was gone. She even chanced a little eye-contact, allowing her gaze for a moment to return his. Then, fearing she might lose herself in the grey, green, blue of his regard, she lowered her silken lashes.

'And will you wear your party dress?' he asked her very softly.

'I don't own a party frock,' she informed him. 'I'm not a party frock sort of person.' She raised her eyes again for an instant to meet his, and then hastily lowered them. For through those small windows he

seemed to find access to her secret being. Through them
some energy seemed to pass from him into her, like a
light-beam penetrating the darkest regions of her soul.

'A black dress,' he said, as though fantasising,
conjuring it from the rich store of his imagination. 'A
wide and swirling skirt. I think it will rustle when you
walk. A low-cut bodice. Perhaps a hint of glitter
somewhere there. And no sleeves, no straps, so those
exquisite shoulders, that lovely back are shown off to
full advantage. Dark hair swinging against ivory
skin . . .'

He was describing Lorraine's dress. Describing it,
indeed, to a 'T'. But how could he knew about it? How
could he have seen it?

Absurd possibilities presented themselves one by one
for consideration, like third-rate vaudeville acts
clowning at an audition. He had met Lorraine in the lift
and she, proud of her purchase, had taken the dress
from its bag to show him . . . He had come upon it
hanging in the office cupboard—seen it and assumed
that it must belong to Cassie . . . Or, most improbably
of all, he had somehow witnessed her trying-on
session—perhaps pushed open the door and caught a
glimpse before retreating embarrassed.

But no, for she distinctly remembered turning the key
in the lock before posing and preening in front of the
mirror. In front of the reflective glass which was not
actually a mirror at all but a . . . window.

'Since when has this been the *In Touch* office?'

'. . . The *Prud'homme* office is down the corridor
now.'

This snatch of conversation came to her like an echo.
More than a memory, it seemed. In her mind, she
actually *heard* it.

She had a poor natural sense of geography, of
direction, but this one didn't take much working out.
Her own office and the one which until last week Nick
Moy had occupied faced each other across the central
well.

Perhaps that should have been obvious, but the fact of it had never before dawned on her. It had never, after all, seemed that important.

She could picture it all quite as clearly as though she herself were standing there, peering across the grey nothingness to the lighted casement opposite, where a young girl, believing herself unobserved, slipped out of her sensible working garb, stood a few moments shivering in the winter chill, then pulled on a dress such as Paul Roth had just described.

Rage and humiliation came to a slow boil within her like emotional soup, an over-seasoned broth. But she kept her eyes cast down to hide her shame, to hide her blushes, and for a moment she said nothing as she ran and re-ran the film, the telltale footage in which she twirled and titivated like an idiot.

She hardly even cared now, that he might have stolen a glimpse of her near-nakedness. It would not, after all, be the first time he'd seen her unclothed. But that he had seen her stripped of her veneer of professionalism, bare of disguise, was insupportable. She didn't know how she would endure this knowledge.

'I'm not by nature a voyeur,' she heard him say, though the words failed properly to register. 'I certainly didn't intend . . . Though I freely admit that I had been watching you, on and off, all day. I couldn't get you out of my thoughts. And knowing you were there, just . . . there . . . I kept wondering what you were doing. What you were thinking. I wanted to find the nerve to come and see you, to talk to you, to talk properly. But there always seemed to be somebody with you, two or three of you in the office at one time. And in the canteen you were so impossible and unreachable and hostile and unforgiving. Morning went by, and lunchtime, and the afternoon. And I couldn't settle to my work for thinking about you and about how everything had gone so badly wrong. I only really wanted to apologise. No, that's not true. I wanted to do more than that, but at least I wanted the chance to say a quiet sorry. Then I looked at the clock and it was late, and I thought you might already have left, gone home. So I got up from my desk and I went over to take a quick peek, and I saw you standing there in that dress. I knew I shouldn't have watched—it was a terrible invasion of your privacy—but I was entranced, Cassie, really *entranced.*'

When his hand covered hers, she started violently. She had been too absorbed with her own feelings, with stirring the bubbling, spitting soup inside her, to take in much of what he was telling her.

'I don't want us to be friends,' he confessed miserably. 'I suppose I want to find favour with you if I can, and if friendship is all you have on offer . . . But what I *really* want, Cassie, if I'm to tell the God's honest truth——'

'Shut up!' she snarled at him, shaking his hand off, fixing him unwaveringly with her gaze so that now it was he who must avert his eyes or let her trespass too far on his sensitivities. 'I don't want to hear it. You're despicable! I can't believe you would stoop so low. You're a common Peeping Tom, that's what you are!'

She was too overwrought to care if others overheard—and, to his credit, he didn't seem to care much either about that, though her sentiments were wounding to him.

'I thought I explained. It wasn't like that. I'm no more a Peeping Tom than you're an exhibitionist. I had no sinister intent, I told you just now. And you're no judge of character if you think I'm the type who . . . you know.'

'I don't know *what* I think. Except that it's been just four days and four nights since you came busting into my life, and in that short time you've broken about every rule of decency and decorum in the book.'

'What century are you living in, for Christ's sake? What decade?' Now he was angry too, in a contained but nonetheless dangerous way. 'There's been a sexual revolution in the Western world, in case you hadn't noticed. Things have changed since our grandmothers' time.'

'That doesn't mean to say . . .' All at once she became aware of other diners around them and, to their undoubted disappointment, dropped her voice to a venomous hiss. 'There are still thousands of people in this country today who adhere to the old values, and I happen to be one of them. When I want to take up a sport it will be swimming or running, not leaping in and out of bed with every Tom, Dick and Harry who fancies a quick one.'

'Oh, Cassie . . .' The sigh which escaped him was heartfelt. There was bewilderment in his eyes. 'What in the world happened to you? Whoever made you like this?'

'Nobody made me like this,' she insisted. 'Nobody ever *made* me anything. I'm my own person, and that's a fact. Now, if you'll excuse me, I must get back to the office. I have work to do even if you don't. Don't worry, I can find my own way back. *Your* turn to pay for the meal, I think. I stood the treat last time.'

She got to her feet. He made no move to restrain her. Rather, he waved her away with a weary motion of the hand.

It was a gesture, it came to her later, of utter, absolute defeat.

CHAPTER FIVE

'CASSIE, darling, how super! Isn't this fun?'

'... Cassie, I know it's *frightfully* bad form to talk shop at times like this, but I simply *must* tell you about this idea I've had for *In Touch*.'

'... Hey, Cass, remember you promised me a dance. I'm going to hold you to it, you hear? You're not getting off the hook.'

As Cassandra Murray, with a polite half-smile on her face and a glass of wine in her hand, circulated among the partying throng, a succession of people—colleagues and guests—sought her out, tried to claim her attention, angling for this or that.

To each of them she extended a few words, making her responses correctly but in a manner so remote, so *distrait*, that one by one they found themselves puzzling over what might be wrong.

And each—as people will—supplied his or her own answer, an explanation for being given such short shrift by her.

'Snooty so-and-so,' thought one freelance contributor.

'I must be out of favour,' thought another.

While John Stirling, bar-room philosopher, man of the world, merely shrugged and said to himself, 'That's women for you!'

Not one of them, of course, could guess the true reason for her apparent distractedness or for the distant look in those troubled dark eyes.

The whole of the penthouse—the light and airy, open-plan sixth floor of the *Monitor* building—had been taken over for the annual party. There were hundreds of people now talking, laughing, dancing, enjoying themselves around her.

But for Cassie Murray there might have been just one.

She had glimpsed Paul Roth fleetingly, earlier on. Even in such a crowd he could not be anonymous, standing as he did a head taller than many of the other men. A crisp white shirt had been his one concession to the occasion, with a necktie slackened at his throat and pulled awry. Awry, too, was that brown-blond hair, which would never submit to the domination of brush and comb.

Red crêpe-paper cladding around the lights bathed everything in a rosy glow, lending warmth to Roth's face, accentuating the high points and the hollows, as he passed across Cassie's line of vision.

At all costs she was determined to avoid him. To avoid confrontation. For she knew that, in the first instant of their meeting, of their coming face to face, the shock would hit her like a physical blow, like a punch in the chest.

Yesterday she had been so angry, so indignant. But some time in the unsleeping night she had felt a softening in her attitude. She had listened to what he had been trying to tell her—had played back, time and again, her mental recording of their dialogue. And inside herself she had experienced a particular, poignant regret.

Lonely in her bed, upset, confused, she had felt the need for two strong arms to enfold her and to comfort her. Not just anybody's arms, either. She had known with the clear-headed certainty of the small hours that only one person's embrace would soothe her.

At four she had gone to make herself tea, and her cats, sensing her vulnerability, had piled on the bed in a purring heap. She would have liked to think they'd come to cheer her up, to demonstrate their solidarity with her, their support. But she knew better than that. They were taking advantage. Cats, after all, will be cats.

They had the right idea, she had reflected, as she drew the covers, heavy with this feline encumbrance, up to her chin. They were always, somehow, their own

animal. She must try to be more cat-like herself. Not
prey to guilt or doubt or emotional weakness.

More easily thought, of course, than done. Especially
now when the need to make it up with Roth, to call a
truce, to reach a kind of understanding, was so strong
in her.

But the damage which had been done was surely
irreparable. No point now in trying to apologise, to
make good or mend. No sense to talk, yet again, of
'starting over'. Their brief relationship had been so
fraught with misunderstanding, so full of incident.
What hope was there that, from such bad beginnings,
any good could come?

'I don't understand it,' she told herself. 'I don't
understand what's going on here—what's going on in
me.'

'Cassie, I loved your piece about the debutantes'
ball,' said someone close to her ear.

Turning, she saw Jill Eccleston from the Foreign
Department, for whom she managed one of her thin
smiles, a courteous but unconvincing 'Thank you.'

'She's very shy,' thought Jill Eccleston generously,
accounting to herself for Cassie's vagueness.

While, 'I can't see him! Where's he got to?' Cassie
wondered, trying in silent panic to locate Roth, to keep
him in her sights, the better to dodge him.

'You look like a million dollars tonight, Cassie.'

'Thanks.'

Thus she disappointed another well-meaning soul of
her conversation, her company and the best part of her
attention.

But she did indeed look very striking—far, far more
than she guessed. She had on black trousers, a printed
sateen tuxedo, and, under it, a wing-collar starched
shirt with a clip-on, velvet bow-tie. Clothes very much
in the fashion of the day, and very much in the style she
favoured.

Smart, she would have called the look. Formal. She
fancied it to be sexually neutral.

In fact, though, the effect—unknown to her, uncalculated—was one of utter femininity. On her slight frame, the over-sized, masculine jacket hung well, without being bulked out by broad shoulders or big arms. A slip of a girl she was, and delicate, under that jacket, while her silken hair falling about the collar lent a note of humour to the outfit, hinting at some whimsicality in the wearer.

Cassie of all people, who never allowed either whim or whimsy to enter her life, was attracting looks from all kinds of men, who fancied they perceived in her those very qualities.

Nor had she any idea of the gentle play of the muted lighting on her countenance—of the way it touched her ivory cheeks with colour. All she knew was misery and anxiety and confusion.

The pounding beat of the discothèque, the thumping bass notes, seemed to buffet her, and she began to drift away as far as possible from the music, mingling with those who preferred talking to dancing, at the far end of the room.

There Lorraine came rustling over to her, a little flushed with enjoyment and from her exertions on the dance-floor. She was extraordinarily pretty, Cassie thought, with those innocent blue eyes and spun-sugar hair. And yet there was a feeling about her that she lacked any real substance.

'Are you having a good time?' Lorraine wanted to know.

'Terrific.' Cassie slewed the last of her white wine around in the glass and drank it down like medicine. 'How about you?'

'Oh, I'm having a *wonderful* time! I'm glad I wore my dress. I don't look out of place, do I?'

'Not at all.'

'Bridie was right, wasn't she? I mean, about getting dolled up.'

'Bridie's *always* right,' Cassie told her, and for the first time that evening, something positive registered on her face—a look of wry amusement, tinged with affection. Women were so much more consistent than men. So much more *reliable*. You knew where you were with the likes of Lorraine and Bridie. Their company was to be preferred any day to that of unpredictable males.

As a sneeze is said by the superstitious to leave the soul momentarily unguarded, to let in the devil, so, for a moment—perhaps by her smile, or by the faltering of her concentration—Cassie seemed to have let her guard down, to have left herself open.

And Roth moved in.

Not, of course, that he was synonymous in her mind with Lucifer—but there was something wicked about the smile which he wore, and at the sight of him she felt consumed by an infernal whoosh of heat.

She wanted to run, but she couldn't move. Not hand, not foot. She just stood transfixed while her insides rose up in protest.

'May I say you look enchanting?' said Roth suavely. 'Would you like to dance?'

Lost for words, unable to respond, she just stood there stupidly, sorting through the possible replies. Even if she could think what to say, she realised, she might not get the words out, might not be able to shape the sentence or the sentiment. She could feel the blood pulsing in her temples, her tongue clove to the roof of her mouth, her throat felt tight and swollen, her palms clammy.

Then, 'Thank you,' said Lorraine, cool, smiling, poised. And, 'Yes, I would *love* to dance.'

Glancing sharply from one to the other, Cassie saw now that Roth was smiling down into the face of her beautiful blonde secretary—and she into his. Such a happy communion they seemed to be engrossed in! She doubted if either was aware of her standing there.

How close she had come to still further humiliation, she realised as Paul Roth took Lorraine's hand and led her away. How nearly she had once again made an utter fool of herself!

It made her hot and cold by turns to contemplate it—
to imagine herself replying 'Thank you' and 'Yes please'
to Roth's proposition, oblivious of the fact that he'd
been talking to another.

What might his reaction have been to her gaffe? He
could have humoured her, played along, led her good-
naturedly towards the dance-floor, turning to smile
conspiratorially over her shoulder at Lorraine, to give a
nod and a wink which clearly said, 'Back soon.'

But then, why should he spare her feelings, when she
had given so little thought yesterday to *his*? He might
actually have enjoyed embarrassing her, might have
relished telling her coldly, rudely, 'Not *you*, baby.
Sorry, wrong number. I'm talking to the organ-grinder,
not the monkey.'

With the blind purposelessness of a clockwork toy,
Cassie started to walk, knocking into people, into
objects, which deflected her this way and that.

Coming, at last, up against a wall, she turned and
leant against it, thankful for the support it offered, since
her knees felt weak and wobbly under her. From this
position, slightly apart from the crowd, she was able to
observe without herself being noticed.

She was able to see Paul holding Lorraine closely,
lightly about the waist, one of his big hands crossed
over the other, resting on her swaying behind, the fabric
of her dress caught up slightly under them.

She was able to see the way Lorraine twined her arms
around Roth's neck. She saw how they exchanged a
word, shared a laugh, though she could not know what
passed between them.

Such a beautiful couple they made! And such
beautiful movers! Hip to hip, thigh to thigh—though
not cheek to cheek, for Lorraine was so much the
shorter, and must be content to press her face to his
chest. But what sweet content that would be!

'I am Cassandra,' Cassie thought woefully, 'and he is
my Apollo. The Greek god, perfection of youthful
manhood.' She remembered how, in myth, Cassandra

had spurned Apollo's advances—and how he had taken
his revenge by bringing it to pass that no one would
believe her prophecies.

Paul Roth was taking his revenge now on her, in a more
obvious, more usual, but an every-bit-as-hurtful way.
And something told her he was loving every minute of it.

She began then to call on Reason to come to her aid
against Emotion. Thank the Lord, she told herself, that
she hadn't given in to Roth's persuasion. Hadn't
allowed herself to be seduced.

It was clear now—oh, abundantly so!—that everything they said about him was true. Not for nothing
was he known as a lady-killer. His reputation was
deserved. If she'd let him have his way with her, as she
had come perilously close to doing, he would have
trifled with her affections. And then he would have
dropped her. He was another Gwyn. He was a charmer.
And he had 'Bad News' written all over him.

'Put him from your mind,' she told herself firmly,
'and let there be an end to this stupidity. Keep an eye
on Lorraine, make sure she's not in moral danger, but
other than that *don't get involved.*'

'Drop of plonk?' said Peter Playfair, coming over
with a bottle, seeking her out. 'What are you doing
over here, Cass, alone and palely loitering?'

'Just catching my breath,' she assured him with a
smile, to suggest that the hurly-burly, the social whirl,
fun though it might be, was taking its toll.

'That won't do, you know. Come on and join the
fun.' He filled her glass for her, then seized her arm and
propelled her over to where a knot of people stood next
to the trestles of food and drink.

'Look who I found propping up the wall!' Peter
announced to them.

'Ah, there you are, Cassie.' John Stirling beamed at
her, forgetting or forgiving the coolness she had shown
him earlier. 'Want something to eat? A vol-au-vent,
perhaps? Or one of these Indian watcha-ma-call-its? A
vegetable samosa.'

'No thanks,' said Cassie, but cheerfully, doing her best to enter into the party spirit.

'Oh, by the way,' John went on, setting down the plate he'd been proffering, the golden triangles with their spicy filling, 'have you two ladies met? I'm sorry, I should have introduced you.' He indicated with a wave the woman to whom he'd been chatting. She was standing with her back to Cassie, and the lacquered head of hair, tight-curled at the ends where it had been set on rollers, was not familiar.

'I don't think . . .' said Cassie politely.

But she recognised the woman when she turned towards her, recognised those curiously pale eyes even as they made their assessment of her—even as John was saying, 'Olinda, this is Cassie Murray, our newest recruit and one of our brightest stars.'

'How do you do,' said Cassie.

Olinda afforded her a curt nod, as her eyes continued to make judgments. Nor did she, apparently, care for what she saw, for there was a hint of distaste in her expression. A hint even of dis*like*.

The feeling was mutual, though Cassie was at pains not to show it. She smiled her most friendly smile and affected not to notice anything amiss.

Olinda Kington was a handsome woman, that was the only word for it. Nothing about her inclined to prettiness, though Cassie could not have said why her blue eyes, her clear complexion, her not ungenerous mouth and her small, almost pert nose did not add up to femininity.

It had to do, she decided, with the inner woman, with personality. The hardness was on the inside, but it showed through.

Oh, and then there were those savagely-plucked eyebrows, which could signal cynicism, frank disbelief, contempt, quite independently of all Olinda's other features, which she would arrange in an expression of geniality. And, of course, there were the eyes themselves, which did far more talking than Ms

Kington ever did, she being the doyenne of that school
of television interviewers who believe in giving their
subjects *just* enough rope with which to hang
themselves.

'I was telling Olinda how good she was last night,'
John said, drawing Cassie into the conversation.

'Yes, you were marvellous,' put in Peter.

'Made mincemeat of the Minister,' John laughed as
he recalled, rubbing his hands together.

Olinda looked from one to the other, and now her
face registered self-satisfaction.

'She's lapping it up,' thought Cassie with some
surprise. It was unexpected in someone so tough and
acerbic, this weakness for flattery. There was also
something in her manner which suggested that she
considered it no more than her due. Very queenly, she
was, as she accepted the bouquets which they thrust at
her.

'By the way, Cassie,' Peter said then, 'I meant to tell
you how much I enjoyed your piece on the debs' ball. I
nearly fell out of bed on Sunday morning laughing at
it.'

At once she felt Olinda's eyes upon her. They seemed
to slice into her like lasers, shrivelling something inside
her.

'Thank you,' Cassie told him rather dismissively,
praying that he would let the subject drop. She had no
desire to steal the limelight from Olinda; tonight she
would be happier in the shadows.

But, insensitive to the sudden chill in the atmosphere—or, perhaps for devilment—he continued to
press his point. 'You write like an angel, you know
that? I reckon you're destined for great things—
wouldn't you say so, Olinda?'

'Unfortunately,' Olinda confided, assuming a re-
gretful little smile while her eyes told quite a different
story, 'I never seem to have time to read all the papers
on a Sunday. Oh, I devour every word of the hard
news, of course, and I wouldn't miss *Prud'homme* for

the world, especially now thsat *Paul* has taken over.'
She sucked on the name like a boiled sweet for a while,
as though to extract all the flavour she could from it.
'But I really can't be bothered with any of the flim-
flam.' This with the same counterfeit smile of regret.

But she wasn't going to get away with it. 'Hold on a
minute, O,' protested John, and Cassie saw her wince at
this disrespectful shortening of her name. 'It's obviously
time you did take a look. Cassie has transformed the
women's pages. You simply wouldn't know them now.'

'Really?' Olinda's tone implied that neither would she
want to know them.

'No, honestly, she's a clever kid, our Cass. We're
proud of her.'

'I'm sure you must be.'

'Don't keep on, John,' Cassie pleaded silently. She
could feel the air around her turning blue, could sense
the chill which had settled like a sharp frost upon the
gathering and which emanated from Olinda Kington.

She had never in her life been the focus of such
jealousy, and she was at a loss to understand it. All
right, she was younger than the other woman by some
years (she couldn't be sure how many: seven, eight—or
might it be nearer ten?). And she was making a name
for herself on that same newspaper where once Olinda
had been the star female reporter.

But television had claimed Olinda now: her experience,
her maturity, had brought their rewards. She could
command a high salary, she was a media personality, a
household name. *Surely* she should not begrudge Cassie
the modest degree of success which was hers today?

'I can't imagine what Roth ever saw in her,' she
thought sourly. Olinda would present quite a challenge
to the opposite sex, she could see that. And she would
represent quite a conquest. But by all accounts there
had been more to it than that. The Great Gossip
Machine, of which Roth had spoken, had put out the
information that there had been, between him and Ms
Kington, a relationship. Marriage had been mentioned.

And Cassie could not escape the notion that they must have been an ill-matched pair.

'Paul, you lousy degenerate, I do believe you've been avoiding me!' Olinda's voice was suddenly almost shrill as she stood on tiptoe and gestured over Cassie's shoulder, holding her hand up and wiggling her long fingers in a coquettish wave.

Turning, Cassie saw Roth a few feet off, with Lorraine at his side, smiling rather sheepishly at his former fiancée. He ducked his head to say something to Lorraine—excusing himself, Cassie supposed—and he came over to where they stood.

'You old rogue...' Olinda's tone was bantering, flirtatious, and she took hold of the end of his necktie and drew him towards her, tilting her face up and puckering her lips for a kiss. Her manner, Cassie observed as she moved a little away from them, backing up against one of the tables of food, was proprietorial, possessive, and when he had touched his lips briefly to Olinda's, she still kept hold of the tie as though it were a leash by which she'd bound him to her—as though he were her little dog.

Cassie, having got it into her head that Olinda rather than Paul had been the one to end their relationship, thought it cruel of the woman to toy with his affections—never mind that he had surely toyed with the affections of many a woman in his own turn.

But Roth, if he were carrying a candle still for his lost love, was not going to give her the satisfaction of showing it. He simply smiled and tweaked the tie out of her grasp so that she was left with thumb and fingers pincered, holding on to thin air. 'How are you?' he asked her cheerfully. 'How are things? How's life?'

'I'm very well,' Olinda assured him with a complacent smile. 'And life is fine.'

The pair of them held a private dialogue with their eyes, and it was not love that passed between them, nor was it enmity—or, rather, it appeared to Cassie, it was an explosive mixture of the two.

She shifted miserably and Paul, hearing the impatient movement she made or the little noise of agitation which escaped her, turned and looked at her for an instant—looked, or so it seemed, right into her mind. She felt the penetration of his gaze clean to her heart. But then he looked away again, as though he had called her up but left no message.

'Are you glad to be back in London then, Paul?' Olinda wanted to know.

'In some respects,' he told her cryptically.

'I was expecting you to ring me.' Her tone became peevish and she affected a little-girl voice to reproach him.

She was a *man's* woman, Cassie realised, the sort who is only happy socially in the company of the opposite sex. She would regard other women as her rivals, would view them with suspicion and would not seek their friendship. Her appeal, then, for Roth or for any other man was not something Cassie could hope to understand. She had met the type before and knew that they always exerted a baffling influence over the male of the species.

'I would have phoned you,' Roth was telling Olinda, 'by and by.' He didn't make it sound like his first priority—the one thing he'd been burning to do since he hit town.

'And I suppose you didn't see me here tonight?' she chaffed him. 'I suppose you weren't purposely avoiding me?' Her tone was playful, kittenish—but whether she came across as sweet and enchanting, Cassie told herself grimly, depended on your point of view. A kitten, after all, is neither sweet nor enchanting to a mouse.

'I honestly didn't see you. Really, you should know me better than that, Olinda. *I'm* not one for playing devious games.'

'I did notice you were rather engrossed.' Still that light, teasing overtone—and yet the words positively sang with accusation. 'Yes, you were very wrapped up in that tarty little blonde, I'm not surprised you didn't notice me.'

'What the hell are you talking about?' Roth asked her irritably.

Cassie, supposing that Olinda was referring to Lorraine, felt she ought to protest at this point, perhaps to demand to know by what right this appalling woman indulged in such name-calling. But it was bad enough just *being* there, being forced to listen to what was essentially a private conversation, without actually joining the debate.

In any case, Paul was quite able to put Olinda in her place. 'I thought it was men,' he remarked acidly, 'who were meant to have a tart-and-angel complex.'

'*You* know what I mean,' Olinda all but spat at him. 'So don't be such a hypocrite. Or would you have me believe that it's her *mind* that attracts you? Are you going to tell me it was her intellect that had you in such thrall?'

'I'm not going to tell you anything,' Paul said wearily, 'except that Lorraine is one of those rare creatures known as *a nice girl*.'

'John . . .' Cassie, unwilling to stand there like an eavesdropper one moment longer, tugged at John Stirling's sleeve. And, as he turned to smile at her, she asked him, 'How about that dance now?'

'How *about* it?' he enthused, taking the glass from her hand, setting it down, and gesturing with a flourish, an unfurling of his hand from the wrist, towards the disco. 'Tarantara! Lead on, Miss Murray.'

There was something deeply reassuring about this man, Cassie reflected as she tried to fall into step with him while he jigged around with blithe disregard for the beat. He was always chummy, always good-natured, and so wonderfully, comfortingly *normal*. She was never uneasy in his company, never felt threatened by him or uncertain of his friendship. His face was pleasant, without the blight of handsomeness. Oh, to hell, she thought, with handsome faces! Who needed them, after all?

Feeling thus warm towards him, she was moved to

confide above the thumping of the music, 'I'm so glad
to get away from that particular situation. With Olinda
and Roth, I mean. I was beginning to feel decidedly *de
trop*.'

'And *I* thought,' John told her theatrically, pausing
mid-jig and laying a hand on his heart, 'that you
couldn't wait to trip the light fantastic with me.'

'That too, of course,' Cassie giggled.

'I thought you were after my body,' John persisted,
'when all the time you were using me. "She fancies me!"
I told myself. "Oh, be still, my beating heart!" And now
what do I find? You've been trifling with me.'

'Would I do a thing like that?' she joked. 'Of course
I'm after your body. Isn't everyone?'

'Alas, not.' He shook his head. 'I was even turned
down when I offered to leave it to medical science.'

Laughing, Cassie took a step backwards and found
herself enfolded from behind in two male arms, while
two strong hands locked across her belly.

'Don't mind if I cut in, do you, John?'

Surprise more than anything made her sway in
Roth's clutches, and as she felt him steadying her,
supporting her, a sense of relief engulfed her like a
wave, breaking over her and drenching her.

'No, no, you carry on,' she heard John say, as if at a
great distance, as she gave herself over to this man's
embrace. He began to move gently in time with the
music, and she let herself go with him, abandoning
herself.

They might stay like this for ever, it seemed to her,
and everything would be all right. There would be no
embarrassment between them, no misunderstandings,
no recriminations. So long as she did not turn to face
him, they need not even speak. What need had they of
words in any case? What had speech done until now but
to come between them? Language, the spoken tongue,
seemed artificial, suddenly, beside the communication
of body with body. Artificial and full of ambiguity, in
the way physical contact was not.

In a moment, though, he did turn her towards him, grasping her shoulders, gently manoeuvring her so that she was facing him. And, after all, this was all right. It was better still, feeling the warmth of him, relishing the closeness.

She pressed her cheek against his chest, so that she could feel the beating of his heart and breathe the cotton smell of his shirt.

The record playing then was *Dancing In The Dark*, and Cassie knew that, whatever happened afterwards, whatever came next, she would never again be able to listen to that song without recalling the moment in every sensory detail. The scents, the sounds, the sights of the instant would be conjured by the music.

'You're not still angry with me?' he asked, dropping his head so that the question should not be overheard. His voice had the quality of some warm, coarse material; she felt swathed in the very sound of it.

'No,' she said softly. 'No, I'm not.'

And, in any case, she might have said—if there had been a need at that moment for lengthy explanations— her angry responses had been no more than a cover, a front, behind which far more complex emotions had been at work.

Around them, though they were not aware of it, cocooned as they were, the party was hotting up. A certain raucousness prevailed and a certain recklessness. As though to match the mood, the music changed, became livelier, and a group of dancers linked arms to form an untidy, high-kicking chorus-line.

Cassie found herself grabbed and rudely man-handled, dragged off to join in, to join the fun. And as she shot Paul a look of helpless resignation, she saw an attractive redhead move in on him and attach herself to him like an apron, draping herself from his neck so that he had little option but to dance with her.

Then, as the unlikely band of Tiller Girls broke up in mirthful disarray, Aubrey Bereswell, with his tobacco-stained teeth and his trespassing hands, seized her about

the waist and would have that it was his turn now for a
dance with the lovely Cassandra. 'You look good
enough to eat,' Aubrey told her with unseemly relish.
The figure of speech was all too real: she imagined
those yellowed fangs tearing into her, and she
shuddered.

'You look enchanting,' Roth had said earlier—but to
Lorraine, not to Cassie, as he spirited her away in his
arms.

What on earth was going on? What was his game?
Was there sense to be made of anything? Round and
round she shuffled in Aubrey's woolly-cardiganed
embrace, with the disco lights flashing on-off, on-off,
until she became quite giddy, until her head was
spinning.

'Excuse me . . .' Aubrey's hands had locked on to her
like clamps, digging into the flesh of her behind. Very
firmly she prised them off. 'I have to go to the ladies,'
she explained, and she ducked out of his clutches and
beat a retreat.

It was cool in the loo, and relatively quiet. The
sounds of music and laughter seemed far away and
muffled, reminding her of those night-times in
childhood when her parents threw parties, when she
would lie awake for hours and wonder what fun she
might be missing.

She recalled how once she had crept to the head of
the stairs, to stand there in her nightie and peek over
the banisters. And her Uncle Tony, always her
favourite, had come out into the hall and seen her there.
And he had come to pick her up, had carried her down
to the sitting-room, where the carpets had been rolled
back, releasing a delicious, mysterious smell of dust,
and he had waltzed around with her while all the other
grown-ups clapped and cheered.

Something of what she had felt that night all those
years ago—something of the excitement, and of the
sense of warmth and love which had encircled her—she
had felt again tonight when Paul took her in his arms.

'I need to be loved,' she realised with the little shock which the all-too-obvious now and then delivers. 'I *need* it. Wherever did I get the idea that I was self-sufficient?'

'Oh, hello, it's you.' Lorraine came tripping through the door at that second, all alight with pleasure. 'Are you having a good time? I think I made a conquest tonight.' And she giggled girlishly behind her hand. 'Oops, I don't think I'd better have any more to drink. I might lose my head.'

Cassie privately thought it unlikely. Lorraine might appear daffy but her feet were firmly on the ground.

The younger girl inclined towards the mirror to renew her eyeshadow. 'Oh, my goodness, he's so *handsome*, like a film star. He makes me go weak at the knees.'

'I'm sure he must,' Cassie said softly.

'And he dances like a dream. I told him, "I've got to go to the you-know-where", and he told me, "All right, but hurry back." Oh, what a dish! I think I'm in love.'

So Paul Roth had sought her out again, perhaps keeping a whispered promise, a tryst made earlier with Lorraine. Maybe that was what he had told her when Olinda Kington summoned him: 'I'd better go and talk to a few people. You go and have fun, dance with who you like—but save yourself for me.'

Cassie looked at the two faces reflected now in the mirror: the one blue-eyed, exquisitely pretty; the other strangely pale, strangely plain, and—so it seemed—quite without charm.

Cassie suddenly remembered what it felt like to cry. How it began with a stinging sensation at the back of the nose, a prickling in the eyes.

These were the warning signals which portended streaming tears and racking sobs. She experienced them now, but she felt no fear that the tears would flow, that she would break down, lose control. For hadn't her tears dried up years ago and for ever? Hadn't she cried herself out over Gwyn? She had never wept since as she had wept for that man.

But the stinging persisted, and the prickling. 'I hope I'm not getting a cold,' she said, more to herself—to the pale, plain girl in the mirror—than to Lorraine.

'That lovely dark hair. Those gorgeous brown eyes. I think I definitely prefer dark hair to fair in a man, don't you?'

'I don't know,' said Cassie distractedly.

'And I *love* the name David, don't you? I think it's my favourite name of all.'

'It's all right,' Cassie allowed. What had David to do with anything?

'David Cox. Lorraine Cox.' Lorraine tried the name on like a new dress, to see how it suited her. 'Though, of course,' she laughed self-mockingly, 'it's a bit early to start thinking like that. Only, a girl can dream, can't she?'

'A girl most certainly can,' Cassie agreed with a light-hearted chuckle. Not Paul Roth after all, but David Cox, one of the junior reporters, had been Lorraine's 'conquest' this evening. And very happy she hoped they'd be together!

'I'll tell you what,' Cassie confided, looking into the mirror still, at the girl with the wide brown eyes, the silky, dark hair, the beautiful elfin face. 'I think I could use a drink!'

'What are you looking for, young Cassandra?' Peter Playfair greeted her as she made her way to the refreshments table. 'A glass of vino? Allow me.'

'Thanks,' she said, twinkling at him as he poured her a generous glass and held it out to her.

'Enjoying yourself, are you?' he asked indulgently. 'Having a high old time?'

'Oh, a *high* old time,' she agreed.

'Seen Anthony, have you? He's getting quite squiffy. A few moments ago he was doing a belly-dance with rolls of Sellotape round his wrists for bangles. Fortunately, Mike Collins had the presence of mind to whip out the Polaroid camera. There'll be a few red faces round the place in the morning, I can tell you.'

Office parties, Cassie realised, were great levellers. The senior staff mixed with their more junior colleagues, and the Chief came down among the Indians. It was one of Anthony Holt's strengths that he could join in the fun and games on such occasions, and still command such grudging respect as the workers accorded him.

All the same, she promised herself a peek at that photograph of him making a clown of himself. She hadn't altogether forgiven him yet for the changes he had imposed on her section.

'Is there any of that disgusting red wine left?' demanded Olinda Kington, coming over at that moment, holding her glass out, addressing herself to Peter and ignoring Cassie. The mauve blouse she wore made a fussy, swishy noise when she moved, suggestive of impatience.

'Sure thing.' Peter refilled the glass to the brim for her. 'I was just telling Cassie here about Ant making a fool of himself.'

'Oh, yes,' said Olinda, and she checked Cassie out with those icy blue eyes before half-turning away to engage Peter in conversation.

'I was saying,' Peter told her, 'Mike Collins managed to take some snaps of him with the Polaroid. They'll be up on the noticeboard in the morning, mark my words.'

'What a hoot!' said Olinda and she uttered a braying laugh. 'I'd love to see one of the pictures! There was no love lost between Anthony and me, as you very well know.'

Cassie was surprised to hear it. Olinda's name carried a good deal of clout around the *Monitor*. She was well respected. Anthony would surely have valued her as an employee? But, on reflection, he would perhaps have found her difficult to deal with. His man-management wasn't all it might be—but his woman-management was on occasion disastrous. And he didn't like argument, while Olinda would be one to argue.

'Get hold of a snap,' Olinda urged Peter. 'Send it to me. I can put it up on my wall and throw darts at it.'

'I'll do better than that,' Peter assured her. 'Look, there's Mike. He'll show you them. Hey, Mike, over here, mate. Rumour has it that you're selling dirty pictures.'

Mike Collins, assistant art director, sidled up to them, grinning wickedly, reaching into the breast pocket of his jacket. 'You buying?' he asked Peter, playing along.

'Let's see what you've got,' Peter urged.

Obligingly, Mike drew out a clutch of colour photographs and began to lay them out in a line on the table, flipping them like playing cards.

Olinda swept her hair back with her two hands and bent almost double to study one photo after another. 'She's short-sighted!' Cassie realised with surprise. This might account in some measure for the slightly staring look in the woman's eyes. She was probably too vain to wear glasses, and maybe contact lenses didn't agree with her.

Cassie herself had no such focusing difficulties. Standing behind Olinda, she let her eyes travel along the line, snapshot by snapshot.

Every picture, as they say, tells a story. One thousand words.

There, as promised, was Anthony Holt, newspaper editor, arms akimbo, hips a-swivel, making a fool of himself . . .

There was the lecherous Aubrey Bereswell, admiring the *décolletage* of one of the more well-endowed lady copy-takers . . .

There was a chorus-line of drunken revellers, literally falling about in helpless laughter . . .

There was a pretty girl with dark hair, in a sateen tuxedo, leaning back against a tall, fair guy, who clasped her from behind and stared down at the top of her head with a look of ineffable fondness.

Cassie's gaze was arrested by this shot of her and Roth. 'My God!' she thought. And 'I had no idea!' No idea that the camera lens, intrusive, had been spying on them. No idea that Paul Roth had looked this way upon her.

Olinda's nose was barely a foot off the tabletop. She was looking now at this same picture, poring over it wordlessly. Then she straightened up and turned to look with almost equal intensity at Cassie herself, the girl in the picture. And there was such loathing in her stare that Cassie involuntarily shrank away.

Peter Playfair, too engrossed himself in the photographs to notice what was going on right next to him, told Cassie teasingly, 'Good one of you, girl. Not bad of the tall geezer, either. Oy, lanky, Roth. Yes, *you*. Over here a minute. Come and have a look at this. You've been caught in the act.'

Cassie was too embarrassed to do more than lower her eyes, to fix on the picture of Anthony Holt and hope to hide the blush which she knew had stained her cheek. But in a moment she sensed Roth beside her, heard him say, 'What's going on, then?'

'You and the lovely Cassandra. I don't know what you're doing, the pair of you, but it sure ain't the hokey-cokey.'

If Roth was as mortified as Cassie at finding himself the subject of Mike's candid camerawork, he concealed it well. Cassie saw him reach over and pick up the snap, which he studied for a moment, laughing with a mixture of self-deprecation and delight—a rich, mirthful sound which seemed to issue from deep inside him. Then he slipped the picture into the back pocket of his trousers, remarking equably, 'One for the family album.'

Of course he was handling it the right way, Cassie realised. With admirable nonchalance. If he'd shown annoyance, started blustering, blethering denials, he would have fanned the fires of rumour and the place would have been ablaze in minutes with the story: 'Have you heard the latest? Paul Roth and Cassie Murray are having an affair. Yes, I kid you not. The pair of them, up to no good!'

Better by far, she realised, to brazen it out. But her

face was burning still and her eyes would be bright from the heat of her confusion, and she could not yet lift her head.

'Don't tell me,' Peter ragged them good-naturedly. 'You and Cassie are *just good friends.*'

'Not at all,' countered Roth smoothly, pretending seriousness—pretending it so convincingly that even Cassie, had she not known better, would have been taken in. 'We weren't going to make it public yet, but Cass and I are engaged. We're getting married. Isn't that right, Cassie?'

He nudged her in the ribs and she jerked like a sleeper, rudely awakened. 'Oh ... yes, yes, that's absolutely right,' she confirmed in a rush. Such a good joke he was having at the others' expense! She would be a spoilsport not to take his part, to back his preposterous story.

'No kidding! Well, you're a pair of dark horses,' said Peter, searching Roth's face, still not absolutely convinced. 'But surely you hardly know each other?'

'We know each other well enough,' Roth assured him, and he took hold of Cassie's hand, lacing his fingers through hers. It occurred to her that she was beginning to enjoy the prank. Beginning to have a lot of fun.

'Take no notice of Paul,' Olinda Kington sneered. 'This is just one of his stunts, isn't it darling?'

'Is it?' As he turned to look at her he gave Cassie's hand an encouraging squeeze.

'Of course it is.' She uttered her peculiar, humourless, braying laugh. 'I know you, Paul Roth. You're double devious. I know what you're trying to do, and I'll tell you this: *it won't work.*'

'What won't work?' he asked her blandly.

'You're trying to make me jealous,' she said. And, turning to the others, drawing them in, inviting them to laugh with her at the absurdity of the ploy, 'He's trying to make me jealous, don't you see? Isn't that the limit? He's sorry he finished with me now and he thinks he

can win me over by flaunting his affair with this little
tramp.'

'Hey, steady on, Olinda,' remonstrated Mike.
'There's no need for that sort of talk.'

'Isn't there? *Isn't* there?' Her eyes were diamond-hard
now as she rounded on Cassie, scathing her with her
regard. 'What kind of girl is she, then, who schemes
with Paul in this way? Or does she really think she has
him? Is she laughing to think she's got her claws into
him? Is she so deluded by him? Well, I'll tell you
this . . .' Now she squared up to Cassie, brought her
face close—too close by far for comfort—and, with a
gesture in Paul's direction, told her, 'This man is in love
with me!'

The joke, the game, thought Cassie miserably, had
gone a long way too far. She was about to say so, to
admit that it had been just a tease at the expense of the
gossip-mongers. She opened her mouth to confess it,
but Paul's voice cut across her.

'I'm sorry, Olinda, you're making a mistake. It's you
who are deluded. Cassie and I are going to get married
and it's damn-all to do with you or anyone else. Come
on, darling, I'm taking you home.'

And he began with some force to tow Cassie towards
the door, she too confused now, too bewildered, to
resist.

CHAPTER SIX

'WHAT was all that about?' Cassie stood on the pavement outside the *Monitor* building, shivering from head to toe.

'What was all what about?' asked Paul Roth ingenuously. 'Come on, you're freezing, let's go to the car.'

'I mean, a joke's a joke,' Cassie persisted, 'but you didn't have to take it quite that far.'

'Who was joking?'

In puzzlement she studied his face, familiar to her now—and yet still very strange, uncharted. He had assumed the wooden expression which seemed to be one of his specialities: he was giving nothing away.

'Well . . . *you* were. *We* were. Just taking the rise out of Peter and Mike and everyone. Pulling their legs.'

'My darling Cassie . . .' Paul, placing himself in front of her, reached out and turned up the collar of her coat, holding fast to the lapels as his eyes solicited hers. '*You* might have been joking, but I was never more serious in my life. You're going to marry me, I've decided it. You *have* to. It's the only thing that makes any sense.'

'Does it make sense? *Does* it?' Her voice rose in pitch, in volume. She realised she was almost shouting. 'Well, I'm glad it makes sense to you. Because I'll tell you this: *nothing* makes sense to me.'

'But it will,' he assured her, low and urgent. 'Just give it time. Give *me* time.' Then he tugged at her lapels so that she was precipitated towards him, and he planted a swift, fierce kiss on her surprised lips. 'Right, let's go,' he said firmly, 'before we catch our death.' And he set her back on her heels again, spun her round, patted her on the backside as though she were a child, linked his arm through hers and began to march her off in the direction of the underground car park.

'I'm dreaming,' Cassie told herself. 'I'm at home in
my own bed asleep, and I'm dreaming. That's the only
possible explanation.'

Certainly the subterranean garage was reminiscent of
one of those regions visited in nightmares, an echoing
concrete vault, chill and deserted and petrol-smelling.

'Hop in,' Roth said lightly, unlocking the car door
and holding it wide for her. Obediently Cassie lowered
herself into the front passenger seat.

Roth got in beside her and inserted the key in the
ignition. 'Whoops,' he said, 'I was forgetting.' And,
bracing himself against the back of the seat, he reached
into his trouser pocket for something. For the Polaroid
photograph which, it seemed to Cassie, had been
somehow responsible for the strange turn of events.
'Don't want to crush it,' he explained, and he reached
over to slip it into the glove compartment.

'Look, I don't know what this is all about . . .' Cassie
began.

'Don't you?' He fixed her with a discerning eye. 'Do
you honestly not know? Then let me show you.'

One of his hands went on a journey, from her
shoulder down her arm, to close around her elbow.
Gently, encouragingly, he applied a little pressure so
that she turned in her seat to face him. With his other
hand he reached across to smooth the hair back off her
face. 'You have felt it,' he told her. 'Even as I have. I
know it, I've sensed it, it's pointless to deny it.'

'It?' she asked, though she knew to what he was
referring—knew, too, that it didn't have a name, that
no word in any language was adequate to describe it.

'It's not only sexual,' he explained as best he could.
'It's not only wanting you for that one thing—although,
God knows, I'm consumed by desire for you. No,
there's more to it than that, it's spiritual too, and I defy
you to tell me you haven't experienced it.' A hint of
anger, of frustration crept into his voice. He was
growing impatient with her, his tone advised her,
growing impatient with her recalcitrance, her stub-

bornness, the mulish way she was resisting the inevitable.

'I've felt ... something,' she allowed. 'But I don't trust myself.'

'It's *me* you don't trust, Cassie,' he scolded her. 'Me personally, or me because I'm a man. I've never known a woman put up such a fight against her own feelings. God alone knows what has happened to you to make you this way.'

'You've never known a woman ...' she parroted him. 'Never known one to hold out so long against you. Against *you*, Paul Roth, and your silver-tongued seduction routine, your sexual overtures and your fancy talk about the mysterious "it".'

He ducked his head as though to evade a blow. 'No, no, Cassie, stop it. You do it on purpose, I swear it, misunderstanding me, twisting my words.' He caught her by the wrist, squeezing hard. 'I've been around, I'll not deny it, I've made love many times to more women than I can readily remember. Sometimes I've behaved rather badly. But this is a first time for me, d'you hear? I'm an emotional virgin. There was never this other dimension before—not with anyone but you. And you know precisely what I'm talking about because, unlike me, you've been there already. You've felt it, been through it, with some other guy. And it didn't work out that time and you're not willing to chance it again.' Almost brutally he twisted her arm, turning her hand palm upwards. 'Well, if *I'm* willing to take the risk, why the hell aren't you? We've each got as much to lose if it doesn't work out—and as much to gain if it does. Oh, Cassie, we have everything to gain ... don't we?'

'You're hurting me,' she said plaintively, nodding in the direction of her wrist.

He seemed to notice for the first time the tight hold he had on her. 'Sorry, sorry.' He loosed her at once and she hid her hand in her coat pocket where it felt safe. 'I was getting carried away. Look, if you want to forget it ...'

'I don't want to forget it,' she told him quietly. 'You're right, I have felt a sort of . . . I don't know what. But you're also right that I've been hurt. Badly hurt. Which is why I get so frightened when you try to railroad me into things. When you pressure me. I can't help it, I panic, and then I freeze up inside.'

'I'm sorry. Really.' He sat back in his seat for a minute and stared moodily ahead of him through the windscreen at the brick wall against which they were parked, as though he might find some answers written there.

Cassie, turning her head, staring out of the side window, saw that a trickle of water had found its way through the ceiling: crystalline droplets, perfectly uniform, took shape and fell, one after the other, spattering the concrete.

'Beauty is truth,' she recited to herself, and the lines of poetry were all at once invested with particular significance for her, 'truth beauty—that is all ye know on earth and all ye need to know.'

Paul pressed the windscreen-washer button, switched on the wipers, and they watched in silence as the city grime was swept aside in two wide arcs.

'What now?' he asked with a note of resignation. 'Will I take you home?'

'Yes,' said Cassie solemnly. And then she allowed a smile to break through, an impish grin, as she surprised him by adding, 'Your place or mine?'

. . . Something about this morning was different. Something had happened. Cassie lay with her eyes closed and ran through the where-am-I and what-day-is-this routine which is so often a part of waking.

Before she was fully returned to consciousness, she remembered everything. She knew why the light quality was different as it washed across her eyelids—knew why it came from the east not west, why the window was to her right hand rather than her left.

And she knew what was missing: the sense of aloneness which usually came in with the day.

She could not move for the delicious entanglement of
limb with limb, for the intertwining of legs, for the arm
which was flung across her. That was all right: she
didn't *want* to move. Ever. She wanted to lie here in the
warmth of her lover's embrace all day and all night.

All night . . . She could not tell how many hours their
loving had lasted. She only knew that dawn must have
been breaking when exhaustion finally overtook them
and, reluctant, they surrendered at last to sleep.

How frightened she'd been at first, how nervous,
above all how shy. 'You're shivering,' Paul had noted
with disapproval as he opened the front door and
ushered her inside his elegant house. 'You must be
frozen. Come on and get warm.'

'No, I'm not cold, I'm all right.' Cassie had stood with
her knees knocking, at the foot of a curving staircase
which swept gracefully upwards and disappeared around
the corner. And she had known that her trembling had
more to do with fearfulness than with the winter chill.

'Oh, baby, baby!' Paul had quickly sensed what was
at work in her, and had come to take her in his arms, to
hold her fiercely to him, to smooth her hair and whisper
reassurances.

'I'm all right. It's only that . . .'

'I know, darling, I understand. Don't worry, just
trust me.'

Burying her face in his shirtfront, she had remembered
how, in the unlikely surroundings of the office lift, he
might so easily have seduced her. She remembered the
fizzling sensation inside her, the way her body had
responded to his sensual taunting, quite in defiance of
her reason.

Now they were to make love: it had been wordlessly
agreed. In beautiful, conducive surroundings, with all
the time in the world and no fear of disturbance. There
would be nothing sordid or dishonest or exploitative or
coercive about their physical contact.

The circumstances then—the time, the place, the
person—were ideal. Yet Cassie had felt not a thing.

She might have been filled with sawdust, so little had her body responded. She might have been paralysed. Sheer panic had had a curious anaesthetic effect on her nervous system. The lines were down between brain and body, body and brain: receptors, transmitters out of action. No messages were getting through.

When he kissed her, her mouth felt woolly, the way it did after a visit to the dentist if she'd been given a pain-killing jab. He'd slid his hand under her coat, unbuttoned her shirt, let his fingers explore what lay beneath. But being stuffed with sawdust, of course, she'd been unable to enjoy his touch.

He had realised, naturally, almost at once. She could not have pretended, even if she'd wished to, could not have faked her responses, feigned arousal, and would not have insulted him by trying to do so.

Instantly he'd released her, searching her face for an explanation—and reading one there.

'Do you want to forget it? Forget the whole thing? I shan't blame you if you do,' he'd told her magnani-mously, though his disappointment was more than he could hide—indeed, almost more than he could handle.

'I don't know.' She could tell how much it was costing him to make such an offer—to give her an out. Miserably she'd stood there, knotting her fingers, unsure what to say or what to do, willing *him* to take the initiative, to perform some magic of his own and break the spell which bound her.

'The hell you don't know!' All at once he'd seemed galvanised by anger or frustration. Without warning, he'd gathered her up in his arms as though she were no more than a bundle of clothes, and had carried her up the stairs, shouldering his way through one of the bedroom doors and dumping her without ceremony on the bed.

'I can't go through this with you one more time, Cass, I'm sorry.' He'd sounded as though his throat were parched; his voice grated. With one hand he'd clawed at his tie, clawed it undone, looking at her all the while, making calculations with his eyes, which had never appeared more green or more dangerous.

She had been lying spreadeagled and he'd come to kneel over her, pushing one of his knees between her legs, fumbling with the button on his cuff, dragging his shirt free of the constraints of his belt.

'It has to be now, don't you see?' he'd said urgently, eliciting a nod which was the only answer she could give. Yes, yes, she saw it, she understood, but her nerves were still frozen and she'd lost the power of speech.

'I'm frigid,' the thought had come to her. 'That's the trouble with me—I'm not normal. I'm cold. I have ice in my veins.'

Paul had seemed to tower over her. He'd looked so very tall, so very powerful; she'd felt small and frail beneath him. Planting his hands to right and left of her shoulders, he had peered down into her face, and, raising her eyes to stare unwaveringly into his, she'd seen reflected there all human desire, a longing which had its roots in pre-history, which was as old as mankind, as old as womankind. For a fraction of a second, she'd felt all-knowing, all-wise. It was a sensation so profound and compelling, she fancied she grasped for that instant the secret of life itself. As though two black curtains had parted for just long enough to afford her a vision of eternity.

All this in one man's eyes? Perhaps, perhaps. Through the continuity of generations, we are each descended from the earth. And in moments of sexual euphoria, we each instinctively understand it.

'Yes,' Cassie had murmured, 'Oh, yes!' with more than mere compliance—with total acceptance. She wanted nothing else than to make love, and she had never wanted anything more.

She had been a stranger until now to her own sexuality, had never even guessed at the existence within her of anything so forceful or so potent. It was as though a sleeping giant had been awakened and now stalked around inside her in heavy boots, 'Fee, fi, fo, fum.'

Clothes had seemed suddenly irrelevant: they had struggied out of them as fast as possible, glorying all the while in the sight of each other's and their own nakedness.

'Cassie, Cassie . . .' Like a blind man whose hands must 'see' for him, Paul had touched every part of her, greedy for information, for knowledge. And Cassie, in her turn, had probed the softness of flesh, the tautness of muscle, had delighted in the smoothness of skin, the coarseness of hair.

'You know how much I've wanted . . .' he mumbled. 'You know how it's been for me. What agony.'

'I too have felt . . .' she responded, knowing it at last to be the truth. 'I have wanted you too, so very much.'

With his tongue he had traced a route from her shoulder down through the shallow gorge between her breasts to the gentle swell of her belly. She had closed her eyes, the more intensely to enjoy the sensation, which lingered long after he had moved on.

His teeth were hard, grazing her shoulder, closing briefly, tantalisingly on her breast, as she stroked his head, taking pleasure in the warmth of his scalp.

'Please Paul,' she had implored as the giant rampaged within her. And he had moved on to her with a groan which sent echoes right through her.

Now it was morning and the giant—for the moment—had been driven out of her, his footsteps dying away like thunder in the distance. She thought she had never felt more at peace with herself or with the world.

She opened her eyes to have a sight of it, to take a look at the new day. The room was pleasingly proportioned, with a high, white ceiling on which the plaster mouldings, the central rose, were perfectly preserved. A narrow window, from floor to ceiling, looked over the rear garden. And upon that garden, while they slept, Nature had laid a gleaming carpet of white.

'Snow!' thought Cassie in childish delight. 'Perhaps we're going to have a white Christmas.' It seemed a magical prospect and a romantic one.

Stealthily she unwrapped Paul's arms, his legs, from around her, and she slid out of bed and padded over to take a look out. There was about the prospect a glistening newness. It quite took her breath away.

For warmth as much as modesty she wound herself in the length of plush curtain which hung there. And she laughed to see the twiggy bird-tracks which criss-crossed the lawn, of which just a few blades of grass were visible. 'I'm in love,' she told herself, as though to test her susceptibilities; to take an emotional sounding. It was an agreeable state to be in, she decided. Very agreeable indeed.

Looking over at Paul where he lay sleeping still, she smiled with a fondness which made her warm to her toes. He had turned over and drawn his legs up slightly. The quilt had slipped half off and his naked back was exposed. Cassie marvelled to see the undulations of his spine, the nubbly vertebrae: she wanted to count them, to know their number from neck to coccyx. His physiology fascinated her: she wanted to familiarise herself with every little part of him.

She twirled out of the curtain and went across to the bed, got in behind him and hauled the quilt up.

Without opening his eyes he rolled over and grabbed her. 'Come here,' he said. 'You're like a block of ice. Let me warm you.' And he heaved her over on top of him, moving under her until their bodies locked together.

'How can anyone look so good in the morning?' Paul wanted to know an hour later, as he made coffee for them in the huge basement kitchen. He had a little espresso machine, gleaming chrome, which sputtered out two miniature cups of the strong black brew.

They'd taken a bath together in the luxurious sunken tub, and he'd helped Cassie to wash her hair, kneeling by her, pressed up against her, applying the spray as she worked up a lather.

There was no doubt that she was in love, she'd told herself. Witness the fact that she didn't even mind him seeing her this way, with her hair plastered to her head and her eyes screwed tight-shut to keep out the soap.

Afterwards he had pulled her on to his lap and towel-dried the shoulder-length tresses, telling her, 'You have lovely hair, you should grow it longer and let it swing free.'

'All right,' she'd said. She'd have done anything at that moment if he suggested it.

'We'll have to hurry now,' Paul told her, setting the *demi-tasse* of coffee on the pine table in front of her. 'You're very privileged, you know, Miss Murray. I don't usually serve breakfast to my lady visitors, I expect them to wait on me.'

'Male chauvinist pig,' she countered. Such an atmosphere of trust had been created between them that he could even allude in his joky fashion to past affairs, without Cassie feeling even a stirring of jealousy.

'Have you got a lot of work to do today?' he asked, sitting opposite her, leaning on his elbows, smiling at her. He was wearing a blue shirt and his eyes had gone through another sea-change: they were the colour of forget-me-nots.

'Thursdays are always pretty hectic,' she said, taking a sip of coffee, hoping it would help to wake her up.

'A lot of people will be getting in late,' he smiled. 'Nursing their hangovers until lunch time when they can get out for a pick-me-up.'

'I'd forgotten about the party,' she laughed. It seemed a lifetime ago. But reminded of it now, she felt the need to ask a question. 'Paul . . .?'

'Yes, baby?'

'You know Olinda?'

'Yes, I know Olinda.' He seemed amused by this rather childish way of approaching the subject. 'What about her?'

'Well . . . what *about* her?'

He knew, of course, what she needed to know. He

took a swig of coffee, pulled a face and pushed the cup away. 'We went out together for a while,' he said. 'I admit I was intrigued by her—she's a fascinating woman in some respects. I mean, she's quite an operator.'

'They say you did rather more than go out with her,' Cassie prompted.

'Well, we're adults, after all,' he conceded.

'Oh, I'm not asking if you were lovers.' Cassie waved a teaspoon around, wagging it at him. 'But they say you were going to get married.'

'Who's "they"?'

'Well, you know . . . people.'

'People often get things wrong.'

'But in this particular instance . . .?'

He drew a deep breath and held it a moment, letting it escape slowly through gritted teeth. 'It was Olinda put it about,' he said. 'She decided to start the rumour. Perhaps she thought it would be a self-fulfilling prophecy.'

Cassie grinned mischievously at him as she exclaimed, 'What a disgraceful way to go on, to tell people you're engaged to someone when you're not!'

'I know what you're getting at,' he fielded neatly, 'but I only jumped the gun by a matter of hours. I mean, we *are* going to get married, aren't we? It's decided, isn't it? After what happened last night—after you had your evil way with me—I think you have to do the decent thing and make an honest man of me.'

'It would take more than marriage,' Cassie teased, 'to make an honest man of you.'

'But we will be married? You promise?' he pressed her, suddenly very earnest.

She took a second to reply because it was, after all, an awesome thing she was agreeing to. Then she told him, 'I'd like that, Paul. That's what I want.'

He spread his arms and she went to perch on his lap, to fondle the soft hair at the nape of his neck, while he dropped his head to nuzzle her breast. Then, gently, he eased her off and confided, 'I'm sorry, honey, but I shall have to get a move on. I'll drive you over to your flat for a change of clothes, but I shall have to leave you there. I've got a story to cover this morning.'

'Oh, and I shall have to feed my poor cats!' she said, her conscience smiting her. 'I'll be ready to go in five minutes, all right?'

'All right,' he agreed in a you've-got-a-deal tone of voice, and he offered her his hand as though to shake on it.

Then he caught her about the middle and they wasted a full two of those five minutes on a kiss—if time spent so blissfully can ever be described as 'wasted'.

In the car, Cassie ventured to ask, 'What's this story you're on to?'

Paul tapped the side of his nose to tell her to mind her own business.

'All right, you rotter,' she said, pretending to sulk. 'Who wants to know anyway? It's probably really boring.'

For a perilous few seconds he took his eyes off the road to look at her, to treat her to one of his biggest and best smiles. And she repaid him with one of the biggest and best of her own.

'All right, I can tell you, but it's a secret really, so cross your heart and hope to die if you breathe a word to anyone else.'

Cassie, obedient, made the sign of the cross.

'Well . . .' He cleared his throat. 'A certain Member of Parliament, one Julian You-Know-Who, has very rashly fathered an illegitimate child.'

'Cripes!' said Cassie, on whom the full significance of this revelation was not lost. There could be no doubt to whom Paul was referring. The man in question was a public figure, a zealous campaigner against everything which he considered to be symptomatic of the permissive society. A champion of 'old-fashioned values' and 'the natural order of things', he was given to making inflammatory speeches which had the women's liberationists howling. He professed himself a firm believer that a woman's place is in the home and under the domination of her husband, and he had only last year tried to push a bill through Parliament which would have set the cause of women's rights back by decades.

He had failed in this endeavour, thank goodness, but the man was, in any case, in Cassie's view, a menace, a purveyor of mischievous nonsense, the sort of narrow-minded bigot who would try to manipulate public opinion without regard to either truth or reason.

He was notoriously publicity-hungry, and would contrive to be photographed on his way to church with his family, or chucking some unsuspecting toddler under the chin, helping old ladies across the road, shaking hands with his constituents. He would be quoted endorsing this or that good cause, using the media as a platform in his crusade for 'reform'. A warm and wonderful human being was the image he tried to promote.

Warm and wonderful, though, in Cassie Murray's eyes, he most decidedly was not. She had even at times wondered if he was indeed human. 'That should be quite a story,' she mused, peering out of the car window as they waited at traffic lights, watching as the pedestrians slipped and slithered along the slushy pavements. Snow didn't stand a chance in the streets of London. She wanted suddenly, passionately, to be in the country, alone with Paul in a winter wonderland.

'It should be a bombshell,' Paul agreed without exaggeration. 'It will make my reputation as *Prud'homme*.'

'Your reputation's already made,' Cassie told him indulgently. 'But it's sure to enhance it. And serve that old goat right!'

'Yes, *his* reputation isn't exactly going to be enhanced,' Paul said seriously, for the responsible attitude he had brought to his new job did not allow

him to glory too much in bringing someone—even a
man as obnoxious as this one—to book. His marriage,
after all, and his career, could be ruined. It was not
cause for gloating but for a kind of grim satisfaction.
'The British people are funny, aren't they?' he said. 'I
mean, they're endlessly tolerant of hell-raisers and
womanisers, they even take them to their hearts. But
they're unforgiving when it comes to hypocrites—and,
for that matter, so am I.'

'I'll drink to that,' Cassie concurred. 'Anyway, how
did you come by this scoop?'

'Well, to tell the absolute truth, it fell right in my lap.
Our Julian's girlfriend, Jane Oldfield, is a long-time
friend of a cousin of a friend, if you follow me. She was
at school with someone called Anita, who is the cousin
of a friend of mine, Claire, whom I've known for years.
She—that is, Jane—is staying with Anita because she
has nowhere else to go. The Honourable Member for
Stretfield North—or, as it turns out, the *Dis*honourable
Member—used to pay the rent on a flat for her, but
now he's turfed her out.

'It seems the poor kid had been having an affair with
him these past five years. Usual story: his wife didn't
understand him, he'd get a divorce and marry her when
the children were older . . . Then it happened quite by
accident that Jane conceived his baby. She told him
about it, expecting sympathy and support—instead of
which he hit the roof. He gave her a small sum of
money, told her to disappear until after the birth, then
to put the child up for adoption. He didn't want to see
it, didn't want to know about it, and would deny
paternity if she tried to implicate him.'

'How beastly!' Cassie shuddered at the thought of
such cold-bloodedness. 'What a hateful man! How did
the girl, Jane, ever get mixed up with his sort in the first
place?'

'She would have been very young when they began
their affair,' Paul explained. 'Young and impressionable.
She was his secretary, you see, and I gather she was a

bit in awe of him. Besides, he does have a sort of superficial charm, which makes him all the more dangerous.'

'And isn't he afraid that she'll talk to the press?'

'Apparently not. Claire says he thinks he has Jane in his pocket—but he's underestimating her. She's been financially dependent on him for a long time but that doesn't necessarily mean she's wholly weak and malleable. Yet he imagines he can manipulate her the way he manipulates so many others.'

'And now he's in for a shock.'

'I'm afraid so.' Paul shook his head in bemusement. 'He's committed political suicide, he'll have to resign when the story breaks. I should be first with the news, but the tabloids will have a field day after that. Yet the man's so blinkered and stupid and downright arrogant, he seems to believe he's invincible.'

They drew up outside her flat. 'After I've been to Hendon to talk with Jane Oldfield,' he said, switching off the ignition, turning to smile at Cassie with manifest regret, 'I have to carry on up the motorway to Birmingham to cover a convention. And then I'm off to Edinburgh to interview Rachel Bellingham for the weekly profile. I shall have to file my copy from up there. What a woman! She's eighty-six this week and she's just published her fortieth novel. I've wanted to meet her for years, it's been a private ambition of mine, and yet, now ... oh, darling Cassie, I'd much rather stay in London with you! It means I'm not likely to see you this side of Sunday night. Perhaps not even until Monday morning. And I'll miss you so much.'

'And I, you,' Cassie assured him. This might be the pattern of their relationship in the future: a succession of partings. But after every parting there would be sweet reunion. Their love would be always fresh, would never grow stale, and she would never, ever tire of his kisses.

'Then next Tuesday,' she reminded him, 'is Christmas Day.'

'Yes, it is, isn't it? Can we spend it together? Just the

two of us—in bed?'

'No,' she laughed. 'I mean, yes. We can spend it together—or some of it. But I do have to go and see my parents. They'd be desperately hurt if I didn't.'

'Couldn't I come with you?' he asked forthrightly. 'Shouldn't you introduce me to them, seeing as how we're betrothed?'

'I'd love to do that. You'll like Mummy and Daddy, they're sweet people.'

'And will they like me, d'you think?' Paul enquired, his flippant tone not disguising altogether the seriousness of the question, as he studied his face in the driving mirror. 'Will they approve?'

'Oh, absolutely.'

'Give us a kiss . . .' He put his hands on her shoulders and inclined towards her. Their lips met and she thought she'd never been happier. Never had life seemed more hopeful.

'I'll call you,' he promised as she got out of the car and turned to wave goodbye.

Pure, unalloyed happiness went with her as she mounted the steps to the front door.

Only as she inserted the key in the lock did it occur to her that she had been sidetracked before she could ask the sixty-four-million-dollar question: 'What happened in the end between you and Olinda?'

'Did you enjoy yourself last night?' asked Lorraine later that morning, setting a cup of coffee on the desk in front of Cassie.

'Yes, thank you.' Cassie, smiling to herself, played with the question, with the answer, flirted with the memory of Paul.

'So did I. Dave took me home all the way in a taxi. He's the perfect gentleman, don't you think?'

'Oh, yes, perfect.'

'And he says he's going to take me out to see a show one night after Christmas. Then for a meal up West. I can hardly wait!'

'That's nice.'

How sedate was the normal pace of courtship! It began with attraction which might lead to a shy proposition, a date, a kiss, a second date ... This was the usual way of things. By comparison, her relationship with Paul Roth seemed to have advanced at break-neck speed. They had been rivals or something of the sort. They had fought. Then in reckless haste they had become lovers. And, with scarcely pause to draw breath, they had agreed to marry. All this within the space of a few days.

It might sound in the telling like utter folly, yet Cassie was as sure of the rightness of it as she had been sure of anything in her life before.

Unconsciously she began to hum a song to herself—'Some people are made for each other ...'—as she picked up the telephone and dialled a number.

'Hello?' enquired a familiar voice at the other end.

'Hello, Mummy, it's me, Cassie.'

'Darling, how are you? How lovely to hear from you!' The warmth of maternal love seemed to flow from Mrs Murray to her daughter over the miles; the line crackled with it.

'I'm fine, Mum. And you? Is Daddy all right? Look, I was just wondering: would it be all right if I brought a friend with me on Christmas Day?' Some inhibition discouraged Cassie from saying more about this particular 'friendship'. It was early days, after all, and she was not ready to tell her colleagues about the engagement, though rumour might reach them by and by of Paul's announcement at the party. Certainly she would not wish them to hear the news, as it were, second-hand, to glean the information by listening in when she talked on the telephone.

'Yes, of course you can. She'll be very welcome, you know that.'

'Er ... not *she*, actually Mummy. It's a he, as a matter of fact. Someone from the office.' Cassie glanced round furtively and was relieved to see that Bridie was out of the room, while Lorraine was engrossed in a telephone conversation of her own, probably with her best friend Sharon, who worked in the cuttings library, and who would expect a progress report on Lorraine's romance with Dave Cox.

'A *he*?' Carinthia Murray prided herself that she was unflappable—but Cassie knew that her mind would be racing as she asked herself, 'Who is this fellow, this "friend" of Cassie's, and is there more to this whole thing than meets the eye?'

'That's great!' said Cassie, not enlightening her. 'I have to go now, I've got work to do, but we'll see you on Tuesday. Be there by lunchtime. Big kiss for Daddy.' And she hung up.

She had scarcely replaced the handset when the telephone rang, so she had to pick it up again. It occurred to her in the instant before anyone spoke that it might be Paul calling her up.

'Cassie, is that you?' The male voice was instantly recognisable—though it wasn't soft or breathy or even a little husky. It wasn't Paul.

'Keith!' exclaimed Cassie. 'Keith Layton, as I live and breathe! How are you? *Where* are you? What do you want?' For she hadn't seen him since her university days.

'I'm fine,' her old chum assured her, 'and I'm not a million miles away. A stone's throw, in fact, depending, of course, on who's throwing the stone. I'm on the Street of Shame. Just a few doors down from you. Got myself a job, haven't I, on the *Inquirer*.'

'Why, you crafty beggar! How did you manage to worm your way in there?' Cassie's smile threatened to split her face. In the old days, she and Keith had been friendly rivals, desperately competitive, each judged by their tutors to be as clever as the other, both tipped to go far. Cassie had known that Keith would be not a little envious when she landed her plum job on the *Sunday Monitor*. Now he was ringing her to boast that he was similarly successful.

'I'm on the *Pendragon* section,' he bragged. 'Assistant diary editor. So what do you think of that?'

'I think it's wonderful news—for the *Monitor*.' Bad news, in other words, for the opposition, for the *Inquirer*. Cassie had no intention of letting him know— at least, not yet—how impressed she was. The *Inquirer*'s diary page, *Pendragon*, commanded much the same respect among the masses as did *Prud'homme*, although both Nick Moy and Paul Roth in his turn were better journalists and more stylish writers than the *Inquirer*'s Piers Simpson, and the *Monitor* was generally acknowledged by those in the know to have the edge in terms of both accuracy and acuity.

'I see you've lost none of your acid wit,' Keith joked. 'I thought age might have mellowed you.'

'Neither mellowed nor withered. And neither has it staled my infinite variety.'

'Glad to hear it. Anyway, I was wondering if you fancied meeting up for a spot of lunch. For old times' sake.'

'That would be lovely,' she assured him. It would be a delightful diversion in a day which promised little excitement—a day without Paul. Her pages were down with the printers already; the work was well in hand. And she wouldn't be sorry to get out of the building for a while.

'I'll book a table, shall I? Where d'you fancy? How about Joe Allen's?'

'If you can get a table there, then yes,' she agreed. 'But they'll probably be booked solid.'

'I'll see what I can do. And, in any case, I'll meet you down in the lobby of your building. One o'clock suit you?'

'That will be fine.'

Her smile stayed with her a full two minutes after she replaced the receiver.

'So how's life treating you?' Keith leaned across the table to pour a glass of wine for Cassie, refusing to stay

his hand when she gestured 'enough'. 'It's Christmas,
after all,' he said persuasively.

'Christmas or not . . . oh, what the heck? Anyway, it's
good to see you, really it is.'

'And to see you.'

They raised their glasses, toasted each other, Cassie
thinking it was great fun to meet up with him after so
long. He was a good-looking young man, whose
roguish expression was an index to his character. A
likable rascal, she considered him, and she was fond of
him, though she had never felt attracted to him in any
sexual way.

'I saw an old friend of yours the other day,' Keith
told her.

'Really?' She raised an eyebrow in enquiry.

'Yes, I ran into him at Victoria Station. Gwyn Evans.
Remember him?'

'Oh, Gwyn,' she heard herself replying casually, as
she looked up at the blackboard on which was chalked
the day's menu. 'How is he?'

'He's not bad. Quite well. Doesn't have a job at the
moment. Well, you know, he always was a bit of a
waster. He's drawing the dole, living in a squat south of
the river, still scribbling his interminable doggerel.
Asked me if I'd seen you.'

'He did? How nice.' Cassie, glancing at Keith,
perceived that he was checking her out—maybe trying
to discover if she was still in love with the guy who had
broken her heart. Mere curiosity would be his motive;
common-or-garden nosiness. If Keith Layton had a
weakness it was his insatiable appetite for intrigue. The
quality was somewhat less than endearing in him as a
person—but for a newspaper diary contributor it would
be a valuable attribute.

Well, at this moment he was to be disappointed. No
pain, no anger, no bitterness or even a flicker of interest
would show in Cassie's eyes. Simply, she felt none of
these things. Felt nothing at all. The ghost of Gwyn
Evans had been laid for her for ever.

'What do you fancy to eat?' she wanted to know. She
had an appetite herself right now—for food. 'I'm going
to have some of their black bean soup, and then a
Caesar salad with a baked potato and soured cream. All
wickedly fattening, but then, as you say, it's Christmas.'

Cassie sat back and looked around with interest to
see if she recognised famous or familiar faces. The
restaurant, on the fringe of fashionable Covent Garden,
was a popular haunt of media people, as well as
attracting the occasional *real* celebrity.

Today, disappointingly, it was packed out with the
usual *hoi polloi*, people in publishing and advertising,
with not a rock star or an actor or an opera singer in
sight.

Ah, but wait! For sitting there, just two tables away,
was the newsreader Alex Aird! Positioned as she was,
Cassie could not identify his companion, but when she
twisted slightly in her seat, crossing one leg over the
other, she was able to steal a sly glimpse of the woman
in the elegant grey dress. A woman in her mid-thirties,
whose lacquered hair curled rigidly up at the ends
where it had been set on rollers.

For an instant, two cold blue eyes seemed to engage
Cassie's brown ones and to issue a challenge.

Or had she imagined it, Cassie wondered as she
turned hastily back to Keith. Might she yet hope to
escape the notice of this person, whom she knew to be
short-sighted?

The last thing she needed here, now, today, was an
encounter with Olinda Kington.

Then, of course, she might herself have been
mistaken. There must be hundreds—thousands—of
women like Ms Kington. Well turned out, with steely
eyes and stiff hair and stiff faces. Not thousands of
women, though, with that distinctive, braying laugh,
which suddenly cut across her conversation with Keith,
distracting Cassie so that she had to ask him to repeat
what he'd just said.

'I was asking,' he told her with some irritation, 'if

you had any good stories coming up. Any block-busters, you know. Any major scoops.'

Cassie played with her knife, spinning it on the table-top, remembering how they used to play a game at school, thinking up audacious 'dares', ordeals, deeds which must be carried out by the unfortunate person at whom the knife blade pointed when it came to a stop.

'If it points this way,' Cassie told herself, 'I shall get up and go across to Olinda Kington and ask her how she is. I shall look her straight in the eye without flinching and let her know she's met her match in me.'

The knife came to a stop, the blade pointing towards Keith. Cassie breathed a sigh of relief. 'Really,' she scolded, 'you should know better than to ask me things like that! Or do you imagine I'm naïve enough to blurt out all our plans, give you ideas for your wretched *Pendragon* column?'

'Well, it was worth a try,' he chuckled.

'Yes, I'm sure you must get pretty desperate,' she needled him, 'having to serve up the *Monitor*'s warmed-over news week after week.'

The waiter interrupted their verbal thrust and parry, coming to take their order for lunch, and after he had gone they lapsed into cosy reminiscence, calling up experiences from their university days, laughing to think how young, how green, how foolish, they had been.

'It really has been such fun,' Cassie told Keith at last, as they sat over coffee. 'It's great to see you again.'

'And you,' he assured her.

'I shall have to pop out to the loo,' she informed him. 'But I won't be a minute.'

'You're just hoping to avoid paying the bill,' he said wickedly. 'You think if you lurk out there for long enough, I'll just pay up.'

'You'd better do!' she retorted. '*You* invited *me*, after all. In any case, if I know you, you'll be sure to charge it to expenses.'

She must be growing up, she thought, learning at last.

Just days ago she would have been reaching neurotically for her purse, insisting she put in her five-penny-worth. Roth, it was, who had taught her to be gracious enough sometimes to take as well as to give.

'Now, that's an idea!' Keith ribbed her. 'I'll put it down to exes: "Lunch with mole from the *Sunday Monitor*".'

'Mole indeed!' she threw back at him with a derisive laugh. 'As if you'd ever get any trade secrets out of me! I'm the very soul of discretion.' Then she stood up, pretending great hauteur, and set off towards the ladies, her footsteps ringing on the tiled floor.

As she reached the door and lifted her hand to push it, it was suddenly flung open by someone on the inside, causing Cassie to jump and utter a little exclamation of surprise, then to laugh at herself good-humouredly.

The woman on the other side, however, was not inclined to laugh with her. She wore an expression of such loathing and spite, that Cassie's smile froze, and the apology she had been about to offer died on her lips.

Fine eyebrows came together above narrowed blue eyes. Olinda's gaze was more than ever cold and calculating, leaving Cassie in no doubt that she was bent on terrible revenge.

CHAPTER SEVEN

It had snowed again in the night. Cassie, lying snug in her bed on Sunday morning, knew this before she even opened her eyes.

It was the sounds from outside—or the absence of sound—which gave it away. All the street noises were strangely muffled, muted, absorbed by the white blanket which lay over everything. Footfalls were dulled, car tyres swished softly. The milkman, cheerful in spite of everything, whistled as he went about his round: the fluting notes rang clear but did not linger, as though they froze to death in the cold air.

Her first thought was for Paul. Perhaps every day, ever after, he would be the one thing on her mind as she awoke. And most days, of course, he would actually *be* there, warm beside her, warm to the touch.

Was he miserable now, alone, up in Scotland, in the featureless hotel he had described to her on the telephone yesterday? Were the roads passable? Could he get about? Most important, would he be able to get back safely to London?

It was unthinkable that the weather should keep him away from her—hundreds of miles away across the border. Unthinkable that Nature should choose so soon to interfere in their relationship. Why could she not have gone with him? A delicious prospect it would be, to find themselves snowed in together, cut off from the rest of the world!

'How have you been getting on?' she'd asked him.

And, 'Terrific!' he'd assured her. 'The Jane Oldfield story is hot! It will really put the cat among the pigeons. I'll tell you the gory details when I see you, if you don't read them in *Prud'homme* first.' His excitement had communicated itself to Cassie; she'd felt fluttery with anticipation, knowing he was stirring up a storm. 'I'll be back in London as soon as I can,' he'd promised then, and the mood between them had been instantly different, deeper and more intimate.

'Will you call me when you get home?'

'Or come round. I'll see what time it is when I get back. It should be some time tomorrow afternoon.'

'It doesn't matter what time it is,' she'd told him truthfully. 'If it's midnight or four in the morning, I don't care. I only want to see you.' And she had wondered that she should feel so confident, so assured of his love, as to declare thus openly her position, her feelings.

'*I* want to see *you* too. I'm dying to get back to you.'

They'd chatted on inconsequentially for a while, as lovers do, just to hear the sound of each other's voice, caring only little for the content of the dialogue, just loath to let it end, reluctant to say goodbye, even for the time being.

Eventually it had been Cassie who had brought the call to a close, fearing that she might be keeping him from more pressing matters—from the copy which he must write then dictate by telephone to one of the women employed by the paper to receive it and type it up; from the necessary last-minute research, the reading of old cuttings and of biographical notes, on which his interview with the great writer, Rachel Bellingham, would be based.

'See you soon then,' Paul had told her.

'Yes, soon.'

When she had hung up, she'd gone straight to the bedroom, to the wardrobe, to take out a small parcel and weigh it in her hands, wondering for the hundredth time if he would be pleased with the present she had chosen for him—the wallet file in leather binding with sections for diary entries, addresses, notes, which a busy journalist can find so indispensable.

At first sight, perhaps, it was not the most personal of gifts to buy for a lover. But she hoped he would

carry it with him everywhere, refer to it several times a
day—and each time be put in mind of her and of the
love which had gone into the purchase.

Thinking of it again now, she resumed her agonising
over whether or not she had made the right choice.
That he needed such a file there was no doubt: his
current address book was tattered and ill-used, the
pages full or falling out. But did the gift make the right
statement about her feelings for him? Did it, in other
words, say 'I love you'?

Her thoughts turned slowly, lazily, to tea. She would
get up and make some . . . in a minute. Tea and a slice
of toast.

'Will he have porridge for breakfast?' she wondered.
'Or oak-smoked kippers in true Scottish style?' She was
unwilling yet to open her eyes, preferring the darkness
in which her imagination was free to roam. She wanted
to picture his every activity, to guess what he might be
doing. More than that: she half believed that, by lying
there and thinking hard, concentrating on images of
him, she might actually be with him in spirit. Might be
in telepathic contact. And he would know it, *feel* it.
Then by thinking of her in his turn, he would be with
her too. And neither the miles nor the elements could
keep them apart.

'Paul, can you hear me?' She thought rather than
spoke the words. And she listened for his reply, but
heard only a crunching sound beneath her window, the
noise of snow being trodden under heavy boots, alerting
her to the arrival of the paperboy. She heard him
feeding journal after journal through the letterbox,
heard the thud, thud, thud, as tabloid followed
broadsheet followed colour supplement, to land on the
coconut matting on the floor below (for not just the
Monitor, but all the best-selling national newspapers,
were required reading on a Sunday morning).

All at once she was keyed up, anxious, the way she
used to be when she took over the women's pages. In
what a fever of excitement she used to scramble into the

first clothes which came to hand, then go stumbling,
tumbling, down to retrieve the paper! She would bring
it upstairs and immediately spread it open on the bed as
she pored over her weekly contribution, the *In Touch*
section, eager to see if it looked good, appalled to think
what errors of fact or judgment she might have made,
which only now might be apparent.

Over the months she had disciplined herself to take a
more relaxed attitude, to saunter down for the papers
only after she was up and had bathed and dressed for
the day. She had developed the habit of making tea,
then sitting up at the table, leafing through the pages of
the *Monitor*, coming to *In Touch* in due turn and not
before, pausing to read anything else of interest on the
way.

But today it was not the thought of her own section
which had her in a flutter. She wanted to run down at
once and grab the papers so that she might read
Prud'homme, read *The Paul Roth Profile*, and experience
a massive swell of pride, knowing that the reporter, the
author of these pieces, was *hers*. Knowing that he loved
her, that she would have been in his thoughts—
somewhere, at least, at the back of his mind—even as
he penned the text. It was a peculiar and exalted feeling.

All the same, she reined in her galloping emotions,
told herself 'steady on', and went to fill the kettle and
set it to boil. She went to the bathroom to say good
morning to her face, with which she found herself on
unusually good terms. And she brushed her teeth and
combed her hair quite slowly and deliberately.

After which she could contain herself no longer: she
struggled into slacks and a sweater and scuttled
barefoot down to the hall, flinching as she crossed the
tiled floor, to scoop up the flurries of paper in her arms
and hasten back upstairs with them.

SCANDAL OF MP'S LOVE CHILD. Paul's story,
his 'exclusive', had made the front page. He would be
pleased, was her first thought—but hard on it came a
niggling doubt. Something, she sensed, was not as it

should be. The printing of the paper was different from
usual—this was not the familiar lay-out, the instantly-
recognisable Times Roman type face. Nor would the
Monitor customarily use words like 'scandal', or,
indeed, 'love child'; Anthony Holt was against anything
which smacked of sensationalism, against all kinds of
sloganising, which he considered vulgar and down-
market.

Such terms would be far more in keeping with, say,
the *Gleaner*, or even, just conceivably, the . . .

Sunday Inquirer read the logo, when Cassie unfolded
the paper on the worktop. So the competition had the
story too!

Perhaps, she thought with a glimmer of hope, this
was some other MP, some other scandal, some other
child? But the name Jane Oldfield sprang out at her
from the grey inches of text. Another name, too, in bold
type under the headline: Keith Layton.

'I don't get it,' she muttered, bemused. Keith hadn't
been on to the story when she saw him on Friday, she
was certain of that. If he'd had so much as a whiff of it,
he would not have been able to resist hinting as much
to Cassie, she knew him well enough to be certain of
that.

So it must have come to him on Friday afternoon, or
even on Saturday, through sources, contacts of his own.

Paul would be disappointed, she told herself, but he
would also be philosophical. She wished then, most
fervently, that he might be there with her, so that she
could smile at him and give his hand a squeeze and tell
him 'Bad luck'.

But the Sunday profile, the interview with Rachel
Bellingham, would surely be more important to Roth
than the retailing of gossip. With clumsy fingers she
turned to the page in the Review section—the page
which had been poached from *In Touch*; the page she
had so recently, so bitterly begrudged him—and she
began to read with keen interest the account of Roth's
meeting with this very great old lady.

Oh, but he was a writer of so much class! So much skill! She was lost in admiration for him. There were very few people, Cassie knew, who could turn out such prose—turn it out, indeed, in a matter of a few hours, in a strange hotel room, with a deadline looming. Yet none of the pressures under which he had been working told on the piece.

He seemed almost to have painted a picture, perfect in its perspective, in its composition, in its use of colour and light and shade. Or he had worked a rich tapestry of words, to portray character and genius and gritty old age.

When she finally laid the paper down, it was with a sense of absolute satisfaction because the article had been all that she, the reader, might have hoped. And she sighed a little to think that she must work long and hard on her own writing if she was ever to be capable of such fine art.

If only Paul would ring her now, this minute, she would be able to tell him some of what she felt! Inevitably, as the hours passed, as the day passed, the sentiment would pale a little so that she would be less able adequately to express it. It was like everything else—like coming to the end of a good book or of an absorbing film: it might leave you a little high, but all too soon you had to come down. Then, if people asked you how you had enjoyed it, words like 'very good' and 'great' would trip off your tongue, but you would somehow not be able to explain how it had touched you deep down, would not be able to voice it unself-consciously and with passion as you might have done in the emotional afterglow.

Thd idea came to her that she should ring him at his hotel. Yes, that would be best! She'd call him up and blurt out a little of the feelings which filled her up to bursting. It would come straight from the heart without being sieved through the head, and would be the more gratifying to him for that.

But when she checked the code and dialled the

number—dialled it three times before she was finally connected—it was to be told by the snooty and unhelpful young woman at the other end that Mr Roth had already checked out, and no, she couldn't say for sure what time he had left.

There might be no way then of contacting him. No way of guessing how far he would have come on his homeward journey, or when he might eventually arrive.

It was perhaps surprising, Cassie thought, that he hadn't given her a call before setting off. But then, maybe he had started out very early; he might not have wanted to disturb her, preferring to let her sleep. He might stop en route and call her from a phone box. Or he could have decided to surprise her—to turn up on the doorstep and take her in his arms.

Wherever he was now, of one thing she could be certain: it would not be so very long before he was back with her, and every hour which went by brought him closer.

Three o'clock came. Four, five, six . . . He would be so cold, so tired, Cassie thought. And he might be hungry. She had bought in a little food with this in mind, and decided to make a curry in case he arrived there ravenous and frozen to the bone.

She switched on the radio to hear the weather forecast. More snow was forecast, but the roads, she learned, were passable. Motorists were advised to drive with caution.

Seven o'clock came. Eight, nine, he would surely turn up at any minute. Cassie went to the bathroom and painted her fingernails to discourage herself from biting them. She had a mounting sense of angst, of anguish. Something terrible had happened! This was what loving someone meant: you suffered. When you had only yourself, your worry was reduced, restricted, manageable. Caring for another human being in the way she cared for Paul seemed to be stretching her emotions to the limit.

The day rolled relentlessly on into night.

At eleven o'clock she called the office. No, the night security man told her in tones which clearly conveyed that he thought her quite unhinged, there were no journalists in the building right now. It was locked up. She should try again in the morning at around ten.

He would have a telephone at home, at the house, in Hackney! The simple idea came up and hit her like the handle of a rake when the head is trodden on. She picked up the directory, L to R, and leafed through the pages, running her finger down the short list of Roths.

Her hand was shaking slightly as she dialled the number. A few miles away, she thought as she stood clutching the receiver to her ear, there was an elegant Georgian square, a tall white house, its windows dark, its rooms unpeopled, and a telephone was ringing and ringing in the emptiness.

She hung up.

He'd stopped over somewhere, she told herself. Tired out, he had decided to book into a motel on the road between Edinburgh and London. But how selfish of him not to let her know! How thoughtless! How absolutely typical of a man!

And what did it mean, this thoughtlessness, if not that he didn't really care? What other possible rationalisation? She'd been led on once again and shamelessly by a member of the opposite sex. How could she have been such a fool?

In the far distance she heard the church clock strike midnight.

She was visited by the vision of an accident. Police sirens, ambulances, walkie-talkies and blue flashing lights.

No, no, not Paul! He had too much to live for.

He'd had a *slight* accident, then; sustained minor injuries. She tried this next hypothesis on herself. He'd been taken to hospital concussed. He didn't for the moment know where he was, but soon he would be restored to consciousness and would call for a telephone.

It meant, at least, that he might have told the truth. It meant that he might yet love her.

And the church clock dropped a single leaden chime into the dark pool of the night.

'You look terrible!' Lorraine told Cassie when she came late and flustered into the office on Monday morning.

'Thanks very much,' Cassie snarled at her. She'd spent the best part of an hour trying to make herself fit for the day, to disguise with highlighting cream the dark circles under her eyes, to warm up her pale face with the application of blusher. But all, it would appear, to no avail.

'Oh, I didn't mean . . .' Lorraine was visibly upset to be thus spoken to. 'I was afraid you might not be well, I thought you might have caught a cold. You look a bit white, that's all.'

'I'm quite well; thanks anyway.' Cassie went and set her handbag down on her desk, unwound her scarf, unbuttoned her coat. 'We'll have a bit of a sort-out this morning,' she told her secretary more kindly, ashamed of herself, of her outburst. Lorraine, after all, was not to blame if she chose, with unerring bad judgment, to fall for men who screwed her up so badly. 'There's a few letters to knock off, and a bit of filing. Then you can go. Leave at lunchtime. I expect you have some last-minute shopping to do.'

It was, after all—though she had almost forgotten it—Christmas Eve.

'That's all right,' said Lorraine. 'I can stay as long as I'm needed. But we can't do the letters now because Anthony wants to see you.'

'Anthony?'

'The Editor,' Lorraine elucidated, as though there might have been any number of Anthonys making claims on Cassie's time.

'What does he want?'

'I don't know, I'm sorry. Barbara rang through.'

'Did she? Well, I dare say it can wait. I'll have a cup

of black coffee first, see if it will wake me up a bit.' For Cassie's head buzzed with lack of sleep.

'Er ... I wouldn't do that,' Lorraine counselled awkwardly. 'I mean, it's up to you, but Barbara sounded sort of serious.'

'Serious?'

'Well, you know ... grim.'

'Oh dear!' Cassie's insides gave a little lurch. Was she to be hauled over the coals for something? Had there been some kind of trouble arising out of her pages yesterday? Had she libelled anyone? Had there been a complaint? If so, it would have to be of a fairly drastic nature, if Ant meant to confront her with it today, rather than let it wait until after the break. The rest of the staff would be in celebratory mood, and precious little real work might be accomplished around the building. Christmas was no time to hold a post mortem. And—though the Editor could not have known it—Cassie could not have felt less equal to confrontation.

Cassie smoothed her skirt, feeling the movement of her hips as she measured her stride, affecting confidence, resisting the urge to hurry, to go headlong into the ordeal and get it over with. Did she look all right? Tidy, at least? She felt harrowed by worry, tiredness, disappointment—but would Anthony notice?

'Hello,' she said, entering the outer office, crossing to stand by Barbara's desk. 'I gather I'm wanted.'

'Ah, yes.' Barbara looked up at her, and the cold hand gripped even tighter. It was said that his secretary was one of the best indicators of Anthony Holt's mood. If she were being summoned now to be praised, congratulated, promoted, Cassie knew, Barbara's motherly face would be wreathed in smiles. If she'd been called to talk business, Barbara would have appeared brisk and efficient. But at this moment she was neither: she was merely cool. She picked up the grey phone, punched the buttons, spoke into it, 'Cassandra Murray is here.'

Anthony's voice, a crackle over the line, must have

said to send her in. 'Please go right through,' Barbara told her, and as Cassie reached out to open the door, a thought came to her so monstrous in its proportions, so horrific in its import, that for an instant she could not move. The chill hand loosed its hold on her gut, only to seize upon her heart, seeming to ball it up, to work it like dough with icy fingers.

'It's Paul!' she thought, and she was flooded by dread: it hit her like a sudden shower, drenching her to the skin, to the bone. 'Something's happened to him. He's had an accident. He's . . .' But she didn't care to frame the word, to give it utterance even in her mind.

The first person she saw when at last she found courage to broach the room was Paul Roth. He was sitting on one of the low, upholstered chairs, watching her as she hesitated on the threshold, framed in the doorway, a picture of confusion. He was wearing the wooden expression she had seen before, the mask he now and then assumed, so that God alone knew what went on inside his head.

Her first reaction was one of surprise and sweet relief. He was alive, at least, and well, although he looked as weary as she felt, and there were little lines of cynicism etched around his mouth as those green-blue eyes took stock of her.

They were strangers once more, she realised, feeling hopelessly alienated, unable to believe that so little time ago they had lain in each other's arms. She asked him one question with her eyes: 'What is this all about?'

His face remained set; his eyes made no reply.

'Come in please, and close the door.' Anthony's voice reminded her that they were not alone, the two of them, although for uncounted seconds she had fancied them to be so, as she forgot about time and place, as everything but this one man receded from her awareness.

'Oh . . . yes.' Glancing over at the Editor, she saw that a third person made up the reception committee. Peter Playfair was seated across from Ant, at the imposing wooden desk, and of these three men, only he would spare her a smile.

Cassie closed the door behind her, backing up against it, looking questioningly from one to another. 'Sit down,' Ant invited her. 'We have a little matter to discuss.'

Peter, solicitous, got to his feet, pulled up a chair for her. She had the impression that he was aligning himself with her: that it was the two of them against the others. But what was it all about?

'I asked Peter to come as well,' Anthony went just so far towards an explanation. 'I thought he should be here to see fair play.' And there was no suggestion in his tone, in his look, that he was joking, making a pun on Peter's name. Playfair; fair play. Cassie said it over to herself numbly, mindlessly, unable to address herself to the situation, which was as yet beyond her understanding.

What was going on, and what had Peter to do with it?

It came to her then that he was her union representative, 'Father of the Chapel' as printers and journalists call their shop stewards. It was an unenviable job, she had often thought, which entailed liaison between management and staff, negotiating pay claims and terms of employment, defending union members if they were being victimised, occasionally playing devil's advocate when one of them, accused of incompetence or negligence or unprofessional behaviour or even gross misconduct, was under threat of dismissal.

'No doubt you have seen this?' Anthony picked up a copy of yesterday's *Inquirer*, held it by the corner, gripping it fastidiously, fingers delicately crooked, as though it were a scrap of dirty linen.

'I've seen it, yes.'

'Then you will know,' he intoned, 'that an interview with Jane Oldfield appeared on the front page.'

'Yes, but——'

'And you also know how they came by the story.'

The typist's chair with which Peter had furnished her squeaked a protest under her as she swivelled it in her distress, turning to right and left, fidgeting wretchedly in the glare of their scrutiny. She could find no words to answer the charge which she now knew was being levelled against her. Sheer indignation rendered her speechless, though she felt if she were to open her mouth, such a stream of invective would flow from her, such sentiments of rage and acrimony, that they would all recoil aghast.

'Would you deny,' Anthony continued his interrogation, 'that you have an intimate on the *Inquirer*?' How squalid he made it sound! How sordid! The word 'intimate' was invested with vile connotations, suggesting not friendship but connivance, imputing something unwholesome, something vile.

'You're talking about Keith, of course,' she flung at him. 'Why don't you come out and say it? Why make such a meal of it? Give it to me straight: you think I fed Keith Layton that story.'

There was a moment's silence. Cassie glanced over at Roth and away, discerning in a split second, a shift in his attitude, reading it not so much in his countenance as in his body language, in the way he inclined forward, listening, anxious to hear her responses.

'You had lunch with Layton on Friday,' Anthony persisted, though he seemed a little less confident of his ground, and advanced tentatively, step by cautious step, seeking a toehold as he went. 'You were seen by a number of people. Together.'

'Big deal!' Cassie laughed contemptuously. 'I was at university with him. We're old mates. We were having lunch together.' She shook her head incredulously. None of this seemed real to her at all, it was all quite bizarre.

'We believe there was more to it than that.'

'You believe . . .? Because we were seen together? That's all the proof you need? And the fact that

afterwards, somehow, Keith got on to Jane Oldfield?'
This was hardly evidence, her tone implied. Hardly
proof. The conjunction of circumstances did not mean
that one thing occurred as the result of the other, any
more than two and two made five.

'You were the only member of staff,' Anthony told
her, 'to be privy to the story. You were in Roth's
confidence—*you* and no one else.'

Cassie felt the colour creep under her skin. How
much did he know about her and Roth—about the
circumstances in which he had confided in her? It was
unthinkable, intolerable, the notion that the Editor
knew everything that had happened between them.

Questioningly she turned to Roth, who answered her
with a barely perceptible shake of the head. She had no
need to ask aloud, 'Well, how much does he know?'
And he had no need to speak the answer, to reassure
her that some things, at least, were still sacred.

Momentarily she was in contact with him, communicating. It was as though the wooden shutters had
been thrown back, so she saw what lay behind them, so
she knew that he was suffering, really *suffering*, even as
she was, believing himself used, believing himself
betrayed.

'Is that really what *you* think?' She demanded of him,
ignoring Anthony as she peered through those shutters,
challenging him, as it were, to come to the window, to
show himself. 'Do you honestly think I would do such a
thing? That I'd be so stupid as to blab secrets about?
That I'd be foolish enough to trust someone from a
rival paper with inside information?'

Slam! The shutters were closed.

'There is no suggestion,' she heard Anthony say, 'that
you were merely being stupid.'

'You mean . . .' Cassie turned again to glare at the
Editor, to engage in another round of argument. 'You
mean you think I did it deliberately? For malice or
spite? Or for personal gain? You mean you think I am a
traitor?'

'I will not speculate as to your *reasons*.' He held up
his hand in front of him, studied it as though to read his
own fortune, to learn what his prospects might be of
wealth and good health and a long life. 'But we were
disturbed to hear . . . from an impeccable source . . .'

Cassie was in no doubt, then, who that 'impeccable
source' might be. She had a vision of a slim, blonde
woman with stiff hair and glassy eyes and eloquent,
mocking eyebrows. Olinda Kington, of course, was
behind all this nonsense. But surely Paul must realise it?

'We were seen together, Keith and I——' she tried
again, exasperated.

'Not merely *seen*,' cut in Anthony portentously.

'You!' Cassie charged him, pointing a finger, wagging
it at him. 'What is it you're always telling us? "Check
your facts," you say. "Then double check them. And
then check them again. Whenever possible, get
confirmation from at least three reliable sources. That
way you're sure as you can be that you've got it right".'

Anthony, fanning his fingers, began counting off the
evidence, enumerating his 'proofs', one, two . . .

'You were seen by Miles Hillier. He endorses what we
were told: that you were with Layton on Friday
lunchtime. You were not only seen but *heard* passing
information to him. This we have been told by——'

'By an impeccable source?' sneered Cassie. 'By
Olinda Kington, I imagine. Whose word you would
sooner believe than mine.'

She scathed them all in turn with her eyes. Paul,
however, was not looking at her, but stared moodily at
the carpet. And Peter . . .? Peter, she quickly realised,
was persuaded of her guilt, convinced by the arguments
which had been put before him. He was there, then, not
to help her to defend her corner; merely to see that she
was correctly treated, that procedure—whether she was
to be disciplined or suspended or actually sacked—was
followed to the letter.

She was moved by impulse, by anger, to the point of
resigning. 'Stuff your rotten job!' was how she would

have phrased it. But a warning voice in her head
advised her that this might be taken as an admission of
guilt.

So, instead, she rounded on Paul. 'You know better
than this,' she scolded him. 'Or, if you don't, you damn
well ought to!'

He lifted his head so that she could read the sadness
in his eyes, which appeared unusually large in his tired
face. His expression spoke so touchingly of reproach,
regret, misery, that fleetingly she felt only compassion
for him and longed to go to him. 'You think you're
hurting now,' his look seemed to tell her, 'but, baby, it's
hardly begun!'

Seizing desperately on hope, Cassie determined she
must bring him round, persuade him of her own
innocence—discredit Olinda. She wanted to remind him
of his own words: 'She's quite an operator.' What had
he meant if not that she was self-seeking, a schemer, a
manipulator? All of this had been implicit in his tone.

But some things she might say to him in private,
which she would not care to say here in front of an
audience. Instead she asked of Anthony, 'And your
third reliable source? Some further proof?'

He took a minute to supply it. Cassie waited with a
mounting sense of triumph. There *was* no third source,
no further proof, no incontrovertible evidence!

'Well . . .' Anthony began.

'Yes?' She sat forward in the squeaky swivel chair,
scenting a victory of sorts, or at least a tactical
advantage.

'Well, we also have the word of Jane Oldfield.'

On the wall behind Anthony Holt's desk hung a
picture, a Turner, a very poor reproduction of the
original, entitled 'Rocky Bay with classic figures'.
Cassie, who had seen the painting in the Tate, reflected
that it must have been chosen for this room by someone
who had little feeling for art. The decorator, perhaps? A
second-rate interior designer? She guessed it had been
hung there because the blue and amber tones were

echoed in the carpet, in the furnishings. And far from making it seem more homey, it contrived somehow to contribute to the soullessness of the ambience.

Anthony, meanwhile, was talking some nonsense about the girl, Jane Oldfield. About how she claimed to have received a phone call from Cassandra Murray. And how Miss Murray had told her to expect a visit from a second reporter, a freelance called Keith Layton, and how she, Jane, had naturally assumed that he would be working for the *Monitor*, presumably doing some sort of tie-in with the *Prud'homme* story, perhaps going for the 'woman's angle' for the *In Touch* section.

'Do you want to say anything, Cassie?' asked Peter Playfair, not unkindly.

'Only that . . .' She raised a hand to her head, which was throbbing.

'Cassie, please. Is there anything you want to say?' A note of exasperation crept into Peter Playfair's voice. 'I want to help you if I can. If you'll tell us your side of it. Tell us why you did it.'

'I only want to say . . .' Cassie began again haltingly.

'Yes?' They all waited expectantly.

'I think it's a mistake.'

'What's a mistake?' asked Anthony Holt with undisguised impatience. Clearly he wanted this whole distasteful interview over with.

'The picture,' she pronounced. 'The Turner. It's a very bad print. I think you ought to take it down. It doesn't do anything for the room.'

The train was half an hour behind schedule. It had left London's Waterloo Station fifteen minutes late, and had lost a further fifteen minutes along the way.

Now they sat becalmed between stations, just minutes from home, held up at a signal, or by frozen points or a snowdrift or heaven alone knew what. Every now and then the engine would start up, setting the eight coaches juddering expectantly, then falling silent once more.

Cassie was very cold. Her fingers were clawed with it,

and she could no longer feel her feet. The numbing
effect she found strangely pleasant, for with it came a
measure of emotional numbness, so that the pain in her
chest, the aching in her heart, seemed less acute.

The light was fading fast. She sat staring out of the
window as the fields turned blue. She saw how the
hedgerows dipped under the weight of snow, the branches
nodding in the gusty wind which blew a fine white powder
over everything. She saw her own face, ghostlike, staring
in at her through the glass, which her damp breath misted.

There was a stinging sensation at the back of her
nose; her eyes prickled. In some ways, she thought, it
would be a relief to cry. There was no one here to
witness her tears, for the train had disgorged most of
its passengers. They'd disembarked at Woking, at
Guildford, at Godalming, businessmen in suits and
camel coats, full of Christmas spirit every one of them,
shouting yuletide greetings, exchanging badinage as
they slammed the doors and went tramping up the
platform to the barrier.

But, with all the hurt, she still seemed to have no
tears, and in a way she was glad of it. For what would
her mother make of it if she turned up red-eyed and
puffy of face?

Carinthia Murray, for all that she was capable,
unflappable, for all that she could cope in a crisis, had
sounded distinctly anxious on the telephone, when she
learned that her only daughter, without explanation,
now proposed to come home today rather than
tomorrow, minus the anonymous man friend who had
been supposed to bring her in his car, and was asking to
be met from the station.

Not that there was anything odd about this in itself.
Young people, after all, were flighty and changeable:
they made plans one minute, altered them the next. It
was to be expected. But Cassie had been unable wholly
to disguise her distress, to keep her voice level, her tone
cheerful, hard though she had tried. And there was no
fooling her own mother—oh, good heavens no!

'Is everything all right, darling?' Mrs Murray had asked.

'Everything's fine, Mummy.' Cassie had tugged at her hair dementedly to release some of her pent-up frustration. 'The man I love has broken my heart and I've been given the sack for professional misconduct, but apart from that everything's hunky-dory.'

'You will have your little joke, Cassandra,' her mother had reproved her, before replacing the receiver.

Joke! Cassie laughed aloud, a bitter little laugh, then realised she was not after all, alone. A woman sitting a few seats away looked up sharply from her magazine, fixing Cassie with critical gaze as though she suspected her of being quite deranged.

Miserable, embarrassed, Cassie leaned over to probe at the wire mesh of the cat-basket, to whisper fond words to Paddy and Perkins, who had put up the usual objections to being caged and transported in this way, but had now settled down, with an air of resignation, to snooze.

Thankfully, then, the engine started up again, and the train went gliding into the station.

'Sorry you've had to wait so long.' Cassie was overwhelmingly relieved to find that her father, rather than her mother, had come to collect her.

'That's all right, darling. It's lovely to see you.'

'And you, Daddy.'

She stood on tiptoe to kiss him and he opened the back of the family estate car, so that she could load in her cats and her baggage. And if he noticed the streamers, the bright festoons, stray sleeves and belts which trailed from under the lid of her little leather case—evidence of frantic, uncaring packing—he made no comment.

'And how are you?' Colin Murray wanted to know as he backed the car round, engaged first gear and set off towards home. From the casual tone of his voice, Cassie knew what he was trying to tell her, 'I know something's wrong. Talk about it if you want—or not.'

'I'm absolutely fine,' she assured him, declining his unspoken offer of a shoulder to cry on. 'Never been better.'

Twenty minutes later they were swishing up the drive to the Old Rectory, the lovely 17th-century house where Cassie was born and spent her happy, if rather solitary, childhood. Lights twinkled in the downstairs windows. A log fire would be burning in the grate. They were miles from London, from the *Sunday Monitor* and from Paul Roth.

Home sweet home, she thought. She wanted nothing but to curl up in the warmth and comfort, to retreat into herself until she felt strong again. Though that, she realised, might be a long, long time.

'Darling, it's lovely to see you!' Carinthia Murray, in her turn, embraced her daughter, puckering her cerise, maternal lips for a kiss.

'It's lovely to be here.'

The telephone rang. Her father went to answer it. 'Cassie, it's for you,' he called from the study.

Involuntarily, Cassie stiffened. She knew her mother must sense the tension in her now, since she still had a hand on her shoulder. 'Who is it, d'you know?' she asked with feigned casualness. 'I'm awfully tired, Daddy, I don't really feel like speaking to anyone. Couldn't you just say I hadn't arrived yet?'

'But I already told her you'd just walked in. Nice-sounding Scots girl. You'd better speak to her.'

'Bridie?' said Cassie with surprise. And she took a deep breath and went through to the study, closed the door softly behind her and crossed the room to pick up the receiver.

'Hello?' she said nervously, testing her voice, listening for any shake, any wobble.

'Cassie?' It was Bridie all right; there was no mistaking her matter-of-fact tones. 'Are you OK? I've heard what happened. Anthony called me in.'

'He did? And what did he tell you?'

'That you'd been ... you know.'

'That I'd been sacked,' Cassie prompted. 'So there it is.'

'So there it isn't!' Bridie's voice rose a full octave with indignation. 'The stupid so-and-so! What right has he to treat you like this? I think it's shameful, I really do. I told Anthony as much, though he was in no mood to listen.'

'There's been some kind of mix-up,' Cassie tried to explain. All at once she felt unutterably weary, almost beyond talking. She wanted to lie down right there on the floor. 'It's put me in a very bad light.'

'Yes, yes, I've heard the full story,' Bridie said dismissively. 'But I know you too well to believe such nonsense—and so should the rest of them.'

'Well, they don't. Not Ant. Not Peter. And not . . . Roth.'

'Him in particular!' Bridie fumed. 'I mean, he's supposed to be intelligent. I think he needs shaking. I shall ring him up in a minute and tell him what an absolute oik I think he is.'

'No!' Cassie gasped in dismay. 'No, please don't do that. Promise me you won't.'

She saw again Roth's sorrow-stricken face, the heartsickness that had shown for a few moments in his eyes. She thought of him alone now in his tall white house. Alone . . . or maybe not? Perhaps he had someone with him. He might have decided, for instance, that old loves were more reliable. He might yet be showing his gratitude to Olinda for opening his eyes to Cassie's true nature.

'Why not?' Bridie wanted to know. 'I'm determined to let him hear what I think of him.'

'Honestly,' Cassie said earnestly. 'I'd rather you didn't.'

Privately, she did not believe that Paul could be talked round. She doubted if he would ever forgive her for what he believed she'd done—and *she* was sure she could never forgive *him* for believing her capable of it.

'Well, you're the boss,' conceded Bridie doubtfully.

'Not any more,' Cassie reminded her with an empty laugh.

'Look, you can't take this lying down. You have to fight it.'

'I don't know that I want to,' Cassie confided. 'I mean, even if I did convince Anthony that this was all a put-up job, and even if he begged me on bended knee, I don't think I'd want to come back to the *Monitor*.'

'That's utter nonsense! You have to come back, don't you see? We need you, and it's your ideal job, isn't it?'

'Was,' corrected Cassie. 'Now I think I shall simply look for another one.'

'Oh, yes?' Bridie's tone was faintly sarcastic. 'And who do you imagine is going to employ you? Your reputation will go ahead of you. They'll say you can't be trusted. You won't have a reference. No, Cassie, *think* about it. Running away can't be the answer.'

'I guess you're right,' Cassie allowed, but doubtfully.

'Of course I'm right. The only question is, what are we going to do about things? What's our best plan of action?'

We? Our? Cassie, who had believed her tears all dried up, now felt them welling in her eyes, chasing each other down her cheeks. *We?* After all she was not alone. She had a friend, an ally. And not for the first time she was more grateful than she could say for Bridie McKay's unstinting loyalty.

But, as for *doing* anything, what was there to be done? Nothing.

Privately Cassie told herself she was beyond hope.

CHAPTER EIGHT

'WILL you come to church with Daddy and me?' asked Carinthia Murray, setting a cup down on the cabinet beside the bed.

Cassie opened her eyes, pretended, yawning, to wake from a long and refreshing sleep, manufactured a smile as she answered, 'Yes, I'd like to, I really would.'

She turned her head on the pillow to stare through the window, through the leaded panes encrusted with snow, at the wintry scene outside, the steepled pines against a slate-grey sky. She could not bear to look into her mother's face, where she read such anxiety, such maternal concern. She knew that questions were clamouring to be asked—and she felt too low, too sick in her soul, to offer any reply.

'Well, you'll have to get a move on. It's nearly ten o'clock, you know. We'll be leaving in half an hour.'

'That's all right,' Cassie assured her. 'I shall be ready.'

The door closed gently and Cassie was alone once more with her misery. It was easier that way, and yet she knew today she must be sociable. There would be visitors later, a large party for lunch, of neighbours and aunts and uncles, who would expect her to be her usual bright, sweet self.

As so often before, Cassie rued the fact that she had neither brother nor sister. That she hadn't even a cousin close to her in age whose support, whose friendship, might have sustained her through this difficult day, and on whose shoulders some responsibility would have fallen to represent the younger set.

All her life, at family get-togethers, Cassie had been the sole representative of her generation, and thus much interest, much attention, would be polarised on her. She had fulfilled their expectation that she would 'make something of herself'. She had won a prestigious award for her writing, earned a job as an editor on Fleet Street, lived up in every way to their career ambitions for her.

Only one thing now remained to be done to repay this enormous investment of love they had made. Something else they would have her accomplish: they were all watching and waiting for her to find the right man, to marry, to settle down and present them with a baby, another infant bundle which they might hand one to the other, playing a fond game of Pass the Parcel with the swaddled scrap of humanity.

'Well, they're going to be disappointed!' Cassie said aloud, grimly.

She would never, ever marry. She would hide her disillusionment, her disappointment in the opposite sex, but she would know within herself that men were not to be trusted and that love would lead nowhere but to heartache.

Yes, it was probably a flaw in Cassie's make-up, because other girls did seem able to form warm, loving and lasting relationships. But given such a flaw, it would be foolish in the extreme to allow herself to fall a third time—foolish ever again to offer herself to someone of the opposite sex.

'If Paul had truly loved me, he would have trusted me.' Cassie got out of bed and padded over to the wardrobe, opening it and peering in, selecting from the odd assortment of clothes she had packed in such haste, suitable attire for the day ahead.

'You're a fine one to talk about trust!' an honest inner voice argued. 'Can you put your hand on your heart,' she challenged, 'and say that *you* trusted *him*? Would you have reacted any differently if the situation had been reversed? If the evidence had seemed so weighted against him? Of course you wouldn't!'

Cassie, passing in front of the dressing-table, paused to contemplate her reflection, her face ravaged by recent suffering, unnaturally pale and drawn.

'I gave myself to him!' she said tragically.

'Oh, come on! What kind of talk is that? What century are you living in?'

Paul had asked that same question of her, she remembered, in the Japanese restaurant, hammering on the counter with his large, bunched fist. The image of him burned into her brain like a brand, singeing, sparking. She remembered how a contained anger had been at work in his eyes. 'There's been a sexual revolution, in case you hadn't noticed. Things have changed since our grandmothers' time.'

This vision of him so distressed her that she sank down on the stool in front of the dressing-table and buried her head in the crook of her arm.

Oh, but she had loved him! That was what she meant. Not that she had given her body to him—offered it up like a sacrifice. Far more than that, she had given him her very *self*. Pledged her whole being to him. That, surely, had been the supreme act of faith, the ultimate demonstration of trust?

'Cassie, you haven't gone back to sleep, have you? You're very quiet.' Carinthia Murray tapped on the door as she made her way down the landing.

'No, I'm nearly ready,' Cassie called back, lifting her head, to be confronted once more by her own washed-out countenance. She must make a real effort, she decided, to pull herself together. She would put on her brightest, best face, her brightest, best clothes—the flame-coloured blouse and a dark blue skirt which had been among the tangle of garments she'd grabbed as she made her get-away.

She would brush her hair until it gleamed, apply a little make-up, and she would walk with her head held high, sparing a cheerful word for everyone. Nobody would have an inkling of the turmoil within. Even her parents, seeing the change in her, noting the improvement, would be pleased to think that yesterday she had been merely tired or subject to a passing fit of despondency.

Here at the Old Rectory she always wore a nightie, guessing that it would offend her mother's sense of propriety if she slept naked in the family home. Now she gathered the silky material in front of her with one hand so that it should not trip her up, should not impede her progress, and she made haste to the bathroom, which was cold and chromed and porcelain and white. She ran some water into the basin, washed hurriedly, and then, seeing a bottle of her mother's favorite Guerlain perfume, whose scent was endlessly nostalgic to her, evoking long-ago days of childhood when the adult world had been such a mystery, she took it and dabbed a little behind her ears, at her throat, on her wrists. Anything to lift her morale by at least a degree.

The morning light penetrated the thin fabric of the nightdress. Under it, when she looked in the mirror, was visible the shadowy outline of her body. How slim she was! How compact! And how *all there*! She studied herself a moment. Her own completeness, a notion of self-sufficiency, brought an obscure sense of satisfaction. She did not, after all, need another human being. She had legs to carry her and arms to work for her and eyes to see and a mouth to make herself understood. This 'breathing house', this complement of limbs and organs, was all that anyone needed.

A brain to reason with, a heart to beat . . .

When you came to think of it, the relentless pursuit of a soul-mate, which seemed to preoccupy most people for most of the time, was no more than a nonsense.

Returning to the bedroom, she shrugged off the nightdress, and as she reached for her comb, she clicked on the little transistor radio which had been one of the proud possessions of her girlhood, thinking it might be uplifting to listen to some music, though she did not seriously expect the thing to work, to be turned to a station, with its batteries still live.

Cassie wasn't a great pop fan. She had no more than a nodding acquaintanceship with the charts, the vaguest knowledge of the artists whose records made the Top Twenty.

But the music which issued loud and clear from the wireless was instantly familiar from the not-so-distant past, calling up a memory, a moment, which she must relive with all her senses.

She could *feel* Paul Roth's arms about her, recall the joy, the bliss which his embrace engendered.

So inadequate, she thought herself now! So incomplete! *Only* two legs! *Only* two arms! Only two eyes, one mouth, one heart, one mind . . . She hugged herself miserably, but derived scant comfort from this protective gesture. He alone could bring her comfort, he alone soothe her. But he was far, far away from her, distanced by miles, estranged by falsehood and misunderstanding. And everything—the whole shaky edifice of her happiness—had come crashing about her ears.

She began to rock back and forth, still clutching herself, and to hum softly the song which was broadcast over the airways. 'Dancing in the dark,' she thought, was surely what she had been doing all these years. It might have been a metaphor for her life.

How long had she been moving blindly around, executing the right steps, seeming to be in tune, in rhythm, with the rest of human kind, but all the while having no clear idea where she was going?

What she needed most—what she knew deep down she wanted—was a partner to steer her.

After so many years, she was mightily sick of dancing alone.

'Cassandra, are you ready?' Carinthia's voice was slightly shrill with exasperation. Cassie could picture her standing there in the hallway below, clamping her hat to her head with pins, affixing it to the elegant bun which was her weekend, her high-days-and-holidays hairstyle.

'Just a sec.' Cassie snatched up her clothes and pulled them on willy-nilly. She switched off the radio and went careering down to meet up with her parents at the front door.

'Come on, sleepy head,' her father chided affectionately. 'We were about to go without you.'

'Sorry,' Cassie told him truthfully, 'I was daydreaming.'

The aroma of roasting turkey, of parsley and thyme, reached her from the flagged kitchen down the passageway, transporting her to those early, magical years when Christmas had seemed the most wondrous occasion. She hoped, slightly panicked, that when the time came she would be able, for everyone's sake, to eat her share of food. To keep up the pretence of high spirits. To pack away a hearty meal, to pull a cracker or two and—with a funny hat perched on her head—read out a joke, a riddle, playing along with the festivities.

'Dearly beloved . . .' The vicar's voice seemed to float up to the rafters on his steamy breath, to linger there like a genie, a trail of vapour, under the vaulted roof, drifting and swirling on the up-currents as the congregation huddled and coughed like sheep below.

Cassie had always loved carols. And as the organist led them into *God Rest You Merry*, she felt the first stirrings of renewed hope in her belly. Those tidings of comfort and joy brought her, indeed, if not a sense of rejoicing, at least a little spiritual comfort.

The choir gave their rendering of *I Saw Three Ships*, and the notes rang pure and clear in the still, chill air.

With gusto the entire congregation launched into *O Come All Ye Faithful*. And without looking at her, Colin Murray reached out to give his only daughter's hand a squeeze, conveying to her wordlessly so much love and affection, such moral support, that she felt the old stinging in her eyes, and had to delve in her pocket for a tissue with which to dab ineffectually at her nose.

They all sat to hear the vicar's address, and this kindly old man, whom Cassie had known all her life— who had married her parents and two years later had presided at her christening, dabbing water from the marble font on her brow, naming her Cassandra Ellen Murray—spread his arms wide and beamed beneficence at all his flock.

He seemed to symbolise for Cassie a particular innocence which she herself had lost. And yet she knew she was guilty of no great sin. Simply, she had been robbed of too many illusions. She was in danger of becoming hard and cynical—an emotional tendency which she supposed she should resist.

She dropped her head to stare at her hands in her lap, the right one balling up the paper tissue, betraying her agitation.

Everyone now was quiet, attentive, listening to the vicar's words.

There came wise men from the East to Jerusalem,
Saying, Where is he that is born King of the Jews?
for we have seen his star in the east, and are come to
*   worship him.*

Behind her, in this atmosphere of respectful silence, someone cleared his throat. It was not an old man's cough, wheezing, bronchial, productive. Rather it was husky, slightly rasping, as though weariness had parched him and made him hoarse.

Glancing round, looking over the bowed head of one elderly lady, across two, three empty stalls, she saw a figure in the pew at the back, a tall man slouched in the seat, wearing a sheepskin-lined flying-jacket, the collar turned up against the draught which nosed through the crack between the doors. With his tarnished halo of brown-blond hair, and his moody expression, he had the aspect of an angel fallen from grace.

For an instant, the shock of seeing him quite stole her breath away. She had a sense of the unreal—as though he were merely a vision, a waking dream.

Their eyes locked and there passed between them some kind of high-voltage electrical charge. But he did not, of course, smile or wave. His face was set, immobile. Then he got up and walked out without a backward glance. She heard the protest uttered by rusted hinges, felt the icy blast like a slap in the face with the opening and closing of the door.

'Daddy . . .' She tugged urgently at her father's sleeve, and he inclined his head so she might whisper in his ear. 'Can I come past please? I have to nip out for some fresh air. I feel a bit . . . dizzy.'

Bless him! For he did not quiz her, did not threaten to accompany her. 'Will you be all right?' was all he said, softly, as he turned in the seat and she squeezed past him.

'I'll be fine. Don't worry.'

She made hurriedly up the aisle, attracting the odd curious glance as she went, though she trod softly on the stone floor.

At first, when she stepped outside, she had to shield her eyes against the ice-blink, against the brightness of the winter morning after the half-light of the church.

She did not immediately see Paul, but then her gaze was drawn by the footprints which trod the snow between the gravestones—and there he was, some yards away, watching her. He was perched on the boundary wall, with his hands in his pockets, drumming his heels.

Cassie felt almost sick with the excess of emotion that was in her—a cloying mix of love and loathing. She braced herself and walked towards him, counting to herself, reciting the alphabet, doing all kinds of mental tricks to keep herself from panicking.

'Well?' was all he said when she came within three feet of him.

'Well, what?' Each adopted a neutral tone which nevertheless hinted at hostility.

'This is not the way I'd intended spending Christmas,' he remarked, as though it were *her* fault, as though she had asked him to follow her here.

'I'm very sorry,' she told him sarcastically.

'That's all right. I don't mind hanging around in a freezing churchyard.'

'Well, it is optional, of course,' she said. 'I mean, you could choose *not* to do it.'

'I could have stayed in London,' he agreed. 'In my house, which is warm and where I have a stock of good wine. I could have stayed and drunk myself stupid instead. Blotted out the whole bloody day.'

'Then why didn't you?' she hissed at him. 'Nobody asked you to come here, did they?'

'You mean you've forgotten?' His voice was a goad with which he prodded her sensibilities. 'You *did* invite me. Oh, yes, most specifically. To come and meet your parents, wasn't it? Those two fine people I saw you with, no doubt? And how cosy you looked, the three of you, walking up the lane! What a happy insight into family life at Maison Murray! Such a dutiful daughter, off to church with Mummy and Daddy!'

'We always go to church on Christmas Day,' she said defensively, for his sneering made her feel so wretched, she wanted to crumple up right there in the snow and wrap her arms about her head, covering her ears, so as not to have to listen to another contemptuous word.

'Yes, quite charming!'

'Paul!' She spoke sharply, and something in her tone, or the fact that she addressed him thus familiarly, by his Christian name, served to change the mood between them, to pull them up short.

They were both still angry—but no longer were they playing verbal games. The time had come for plain speaking. 'I don't know why you've come here. I don't know what you want. Believing what you believe, I can't think why you should want to set eyes on me again. And, after yesterday, *I* certainly never wanted to set eyes on *you*. Really, I can't see we have anything to say to each other.'

'Oh, you don't?' He levered himself off the wall with his hands, landing with a crunch on the snow right in front of her, so close in fact that she must raise her head, lift her face to look into his. 'Well, I think there are things we *must* say. I'm looking for explanations,

Cassie. For the truth—however distasteful. I want to
know why you did it, why you hate me so much. Are
you really that screwed up? If so, then you need help.'

'You're the one who needs help,' she snapped at him.
'You need your head seeing to!' Once again he seemed
to have reduced her to this futile tit-for-tat style of
argument. She heard her own childish retort with
dismay, and told herself she should start to make a bit
of sense. 'If you wanted explanations,' she told him
more levelly, 'you should have come straight to me for
them, instead of running off to the Editor, telling tales,
laying blame. You should have come and challenged me
to my face. Instead of which you . . . you . . .'

And the memory of her meeting with Anthony
yesterday, of her hurt and humiliation, brought tears to
her eyes.

'I would have come to you,' he told her more softly,
more reasonably. 'But the first I knew of anything
amiss was when Anthony called me up at the hotel on
Saturday night. Or, more precisely, in the early hours of
Sunday.'

That sounded about right to Cassie. She could well
imagine the busy little man—he who was said never to
sleep at night—ringing one of his employees in the
small hours to talk business. 'What did he say?' she
queried.

'He said he wanted to see me the minute I got back to
town. I was to call straight round to his house. He
wouldn't discuss it over the phone. Well, I set off early
and I had a devil of a journey with black ice on the
roads, drifting snow, the lot. When I finally got to his
place in the evening, he waved a copy of the *Inquirer*
under my nose . . .' He broke off mid-narrative to fix
her with a look of such reproach, that inwardly she
writhed. 'Well, I hadn't even seen it. I mean, there'd
been no time for reading newspapers. Whereas he'd got
hold of an early edition, hot off the press. Not only
that, but he'd had a call from Olinda telling him——'

'We know what that woman told him!' Cassie flung

at Paul. 'I don't want to hear it all over again. It's all lies, damned lies . . .' And she had to turn her face away to hide from him the fact that those treacherous tears had sprung again.

'How can it be lies?' He took hold of her angrily by the shoulders and shook her. She was limp in his grasp, her hands flapped at the ends of her arms, her head was flung back; she put up no resistance.

'And why should it be true? *I* say it's lies, why can't you believe me?'

Now she forced herself to raise her head, to meet his eye, so that he must read her sincerity, so that he would feel bound to answer her.

What she saw shocked her rigid, for his expression might have been a mirror of her own, reflecting her pallor, the blue tinge of cold, the lines of weariness and misery etched deep. Oh, the *pain* she saw there! And the pain she suffered!

He still had his hands clamped on her shoulders. He drew her to him so that her cheek pressed against his chest, and he spoke over the top of her head. 'I was so in love with you. Besotted. Perhaps still am. And I *want* to forgive you, Cassie, but I can't.'

'I'm not asking for absolution,' she told him, her voice muffled, addressing the words into the sheepskin lining of his jacket. 'I have nothing to ask forgiveness for. Not so far as you're concerned, at any rate. It's *I* who have to forgive *you*—though I don't suppose I ever shall.'

'Why must you persist . . .' As rudely as he had seized hold of her, he now shoved her away, releasing her. His eyes were as green as they had ever been, dark as the yew-tree which grew nearby, its berries as poisonous as they were pretty. 'Why can't you tell the truth now?'

Cassie turned from him to read the sad inscription on a headstone, in memory of someone who had died a century ago. This icy garden seemed to her suddenly full of ghosts. She imagined they were overheard—that invisible people, spectres, shades, listened on every hand.

'Of course I didn't just take Olinda's word for it. I know she can be a dangerous woman—though I've never believed her capable of an outright lie. But other people had seen you with Layton.'

The way he pronounced the name was a revelation in itself. Such detestation was implicit in the utterance of it, that Cassie knew Roth blamed Keith for more than merely stealing his story. He thought he had been betrayed in more ways than one. Perhaps even that the two of them had been colluding all along, laughing at him behind his back.

'I've known Keith Layton for years,' she began, and then she saw that, unwittingly, she had confirmed his worst suspicions. Whatever Cassie's motive when she'd made love with him that night, she had never for one moment given him her heart. This was how his thoughts were running. She had another *amour*, a passion of long standing. She and Keith Layton went way back!

'I went to see Jane Oldfield,' he continued after a weighty pause, and he seemed to be dragging the words out. 'She was absolutely furious at the way she'd been tricked. She'd talked to the *Monitor* she said, talked to me, because of its—of my—reputation for integrity. She wanted to tell her story through the reputable press. She'd chosen the *Monitor*, not the *Inquirer*, or the *Gleaner* or any of the others.'

'She couldn't have blamed you, though,' Cassie put in, 'if the story had been somehow leaked. It was hardly down to you.'

'Of course it was down to me!' he shouted so loudly that she feared the little congregation inside the church, about the business of worshipping, would hear his every word. 'I told you, and you told Layton. And you telephoned her and told her you would be sending a freelance reporter to do a tie-in. And she naturally assumed . . . oh, what's the point of going over and over the same ground?'

He dropped his head to glower at his boots; which the snow had stained with white. Above them a lone bird sang irreverently, cheerfully.

Cassie took a deep breath, let it out again, shook her head and told him dully, 'It wasn't me who telephoned Jane Oldfield. Whoever it was, Paul, it wasn't me. And I never breathed a word of it to Keith, I swear I didn't. He never had the tip-off from me.'

He lifted his hand to her face, let his fingertips stray across her frozen cheek. He said not a word, but she knew that he believed her—or, at least, that he *half* believed her. That her sincerity could not be denied. That her denials were too persuasive to resist.

'I *want* that to be the truth,' he said. 'More than anything, that's what I want. Oh, Cassie, is it really so?'

Something seemed to spark in her, like a match being touched to a fuse, and immediately she felt the shock of an emotional explosion inside herself.

'I told you it's the truth, and I'm not telling you again. Go to hell, Paul Roth, go away from me! I never want to see you again. I've only known you a short while—but you've succeeded already in ruining my life.'

'I can ask some more questions,' he told her urgently, and he squeezed her elbow so that it hurt, digging his fingers into the spare flesh. 'If you are telling the truth then Anthony will have to know about it, and we'll all owe you——'

Wresting her arm free she bawled at him, 'I don't want to hear another "if"!' And she took a swing at him with one clenched fist so that he had to dodge the blow. 'Why can't you get it into your head? It's not a matter of if, it's a matter of fact. You've screwed me up rotten. You've lost me my job. Now I hope you're satisfied, that's all.'

Words seemed to elude him. He just stared at her in apparent bewilderment, though she guessed that his quick, clever mind would be at work behind the blank visage.

'You and Layton . . .' he began at last.

'Keith and I are old mates.'

'But have you ever been . . . more than that?'

'Oh, I hate you! I hate you!' She pushed him, shoving

her hands flat against his broad chest, but she could not unbalance him. 'Go away from here! Leave me alone! I don't want to have to look at you a moment longer, you . . . you creep!'

It wasn't the word she would ideally have chosen to describe him. Cassie, in her writing, picked and chose her nouns, her verbs, her adjectives with infinite care. But she seldom wrote when she felt beside herself with anger and with her brain all a-jumble as it was now. 'Creep' was not what she, in her more lucid moments, would have called Paul Roth. All the same, the jibe hit home.

If she had read pain in his expression before, and if it had seemed to be a reflection of what she was feeling, it was as nothing to what was inside her now, and what she saw mirrored in his eyes. They had loved and they had lost. Both of them, utterly. This had been no mere argument between them, a tiff, a rift which might yet be healed.

Things had been said, had been thought—or so it seemed to Cassie—which could not be unsaid or unthought. And could never, ever be forgiven. So, although they might in their hearts, at the very core of their beings, want nothing more than to kiss and embrace and say sorry, it would not be possible.

Sorry simply was not good enough. It would not recompense her.

'Please,' she said emptily, desolately, '*please* go now.'

And she dropped her head so that curtains of dark hair hung about her face. And when next she looked, he had gone. Disappeared. As mysteriously as he had appeared. And she was left alone with the listening ghosts.

The doors of the church were flung wide, and organ music issued with the first of the chattering congregation, out into the cold midday.

Sighing, Cassie wandered over to join them where they stood exchanging pleasantries, good wishes, compliments of the bitter season.

'Darling, are you feeling better?' Carinthia Murray eyed her daughter with thinly-veiled suspicion, as she always used to do when Cassie was a child and manifested symptoms of mumps or measles or the flu. She knew her mother's worried frown so well by now. And the clucking of her tongue sounded a warning that she might expect, if she did not resist, to be packed off to bed, to have a thermometer pressed between her lips, to be given a pill or powder and ordered to rest.

'Yes, I'm fine,' she said breezily because, while the prospect of crawling between the sheets, of retreating into semi-hibernation, was not altogether unappealing, she was determined not to mar anyone else's Christmas.

And only when, unconvinced, Mrs Murray continued to subject her to such piercing scrutiny did Cassie realise just what was on her mind.

Not bug or virus, flu or fever, now concerned Carinthia. No. She was wondering, rather, if her daughter's seediness, her sickness, had some other cause. 'Crikey!' thought Cassie indignantly. 'She's wondering if I'm pregnant!'

Indignation, however, gave way swiftly to an awesome realisation—that this was indeed a possibility. She had, after all, made love with a man, and had given not a thought to this eventuality. Such had been her passion that she hadn't stopped to consider this likely outcome.

And the ironies of the situation were not for a moment lost on her: the fact that she, Cassie Murray, had written regularly and authoritatively on women's issues, on relationships, on contraception, on motherhood; the fact that she could well herself be in the same situation as poor Jane Oldfield, expecting the child of a man who was not and never could be her husband.

Never could be? Well, of course, Paul was free to marry her. He was not a cheat or an adulterer. And it was unlikely in the extreme that he would deny responsibility for his offspring, flesh of his flesh. More than mere duty, or the fear of being branded a hypocrite, would demand that he stand by her. For somehow she knew that he would love and care for a son or daughter with a particular, fierce pride. *That* was the kind of man he was, and *that* was why she had loved him—why she loved him still.

But surely it was impossible that they had between them created another life? She was letting her fancy run away with her.

'No,' she told herself adamantly as they trudged homeward. And, intending no pun, no clever play on words, 'It's inconceivable.'

CHAPTER NINE

'HERE we are at last.' Cassie set the cat-basket down in the hallway of her flat and knelt to unlatch the metal-grid door, to release Paddy and Perkins, who came stalking out, tails held high, squawking their protests about the indignity and the discomfort to which they'd been subjected.

'I'm sorry,' she told them, 'but it couldn't be helped.' And, as she reached out to pet them, to knead the soft flesh at the scruff of a furry neck, to stroke an arching back, 'Anyway, I'm glad to be home, aren't you?'

It was a relief at last to be able to let her guard down. To stop pretending. She should have won an Oscar, she told herself, for the performance she had been giving, for the way she'd held up over Christmas and Boxing Day. Even Carinthia Murray had at last been persuaded that all was well with her daughter. And no one could have guessed as she laughed and chatted and joked her way through the festivities how she was inwardly seething.

Now, thank heavens, she had a bit of space to herself. A bit of time to indulge in abject misery, to give full rein to self-pity. She could mope or weep or whatever she wished.

She had no clear plan as to how she might proceed with her life. She felt like someone who had walked slap into a brick wall and was still dazed from the impact. And she knew it would be hopeless to try to think straight while her head was still spinning as it was.

Speeding through the streets of London in a taxi from Waterloo Station she had gazed out at the deserted streets which seemed to confirm the sense of unreality which had settled on her. Most office workers would not return to their desks until after the New

Year holiday. This was the usual way of things—and yet she was half persuaded that something catastrophic had happened, that plague or pestilence had wiped out most of the capital's teeming population, lending it the aspect of a ghost-town.

Not all the workforce, of course, could afford to take so long a break. Not every Londoner was allowed more than the statutory two days off. There were vital services to run, after all, and the wheels of industry had to keep turning, and those in the communications business had to be about the business of communicating. People in television, in radio . . . and in newspapers.

The *Monitor* building would be buzzing by now, a veritable hive of activity. It had always been one of the biggest thrills to Cassie, playing her part in it. There had been copy dates to meet. Printing schedules. Deadlines. And the adrenalin would flow. Now there were no dates in her diary, no goals to work towards, just a lifetime stretching meaninglessly, endlessly ahead of her.

She should be fighting back—that was what Bridie had told her. Making strenuous efforts to clear her name. But Bridie did not fully understand the hopelessness of the situation. She didn't know about this thing—this *fling*—which Cassie had had with Roth. She should not be expected to realise what a travesty it all was. And she would be an optimist indeed if she believed that a shattered dream could ever be rebuilt.

Sighing, Cassie went to fill the kettle, to make herself tea. And she lay on the sofa and pushed her face into a cushion and tried to clear her mind, to free herself from introspection, to think of nothing—since to think, right now, was to suffer.

The telephone rang even as the kettle boiled.

Cassie went and made the tea.

By and by the ringing stopped.

She went to the airing-cupboard and switched on the immersion heater, deciding she would take a bath. It was not yet ten-thirty. She had left the Old Rectory early that morning, making as if to set off for work. She had prayed no one would question her—'*Must* you go back?'—and, mercifully, no one had. She had not been obliged to tell a lie to her parents, even by implication. Unless leaving at that time of day and in so businesslike a fashion, was in itself tantamount to lying.

An hour later, as she reclined steeping in scented water, the telephone rang again, long and insistent.

There was a time, Cassie recalled, gazing at the winking bubbles with their rainbow tints, when she could not have ignored it. When she would have run to pick up the receiver, eager to hear who was on the other end of the line. But she was no longer so immature, and she expected only a wrong number, or bad news, or a stranger bent on selling her life assurance.

She got out of the tub, wrapped a towel about herself, and went to the bedroom for fresh clothes.

The telephone rang again.

'Shall I? Shan't I?' Cassie asked herself indifferently. 'Oh, what the heck? I might as well.' But by the time she got there, the ringing had stopped.

'Good job too,' she muttered, and she took the receiver off the hook, so that the trilling bell could not again intrude upon her isolation to remind her there were people out there.

She dressed in trim-fitting black trousers, a white fluffy sweater, tied her hair back with a length of velvet ribbon, and took from the bookcase the first volume which came to hand. It turned out to be her world atlas, so she sat on the floor and stared at the maps, the land masses in green, blue, yellow, the unnatural azure of the oceans.

Flipping the pages, she read place names—Paraguay, Peru, Philippines—and thought about running away. Thought about disappearing. Perhaps there was her salvation—in travel? Maybe, with the miles, her heartache would subside? She visualised the Equator as though it were an actual line, a belt around the vast girth of the globe. She saw herself crossing that line and, miraculously, finding herself beyond the reach of misery.

Saudi Arabia, Seychelles, Singapore . . . Her finger

went on a journey of its own down the index page, the grey lists of far-away places with strange-sounding names.

Keith Layton, of course, must know the truth. Could tell how he had come by the story, how the contact with Jane Oldfield had been made. Pressed, he might confess that a little subterfuge had been used. He could not know what trouble he had brought on Cassie, and, she was sure, would do whatever he could to make amends, for they were friendly rivals, not sworn enemies.

But then, what purpose would that serve? Who would believe him any more than they believed her? They were thought to have conspired, she and Keith, and this might be seen simply as further evidence of collusion.

'Let it go, let it go,' she told herself. There was no fight in her.

The doorbell rang.

Was she expecting anyone? No, she thought. It was probably just a tradesman, the postman, the gas-man come to read the meter. Or it might be for the people in the flat below—the caller could simply have pushed the wrong button. Sighing, she went to her own door and through it to the head of the stairs, from which vantage she had a view across the tiled hallways to the front door, and could discern, through the bubbled glass, the figure of a woman.

The doorbell rang again. Cassie padded barefoot down to answer it.

'So there you are!' said Bridie McKay triumphantly. 'I just *knew* I'd find you in.'

'Hello,' said Cassie blankly, and then, because friendship and common courtesy demanded it, 'Won't you come in? Come up for a coffee? It's good to see you.'

'This is no time to be drinking coffee,' Bridie scolded, peering at her through glinting spectacle lenses. 'You have to come to the office. To see Anthony. It's all sorted out now, everything's all right.'

'To see Anthony?' echoed Cassie blankly. 'But I don't *want* to see him! I don't want to see any of them ever again.'

By 'them' she meant all her former colleagues—the
male ones, at least—who, in her imagination, had all
turned against her, so bad was her sense of alienation.

'Of course you do,' Bridie insisted, 'if only for the
satisfaction of hearing him apologise. Afterwards you
can do what you like, but for my sake at least come
back for that.'

Taking charge, she grabbed hold of Cassie's arm and
propelled her back upstairs. 'Come along, get your
boots on. Where's your coat? You're coming with me.
Hurry up, I have a taxi waiting.'

'A taxi?' This would be extravagance indeed for
Bridie, who always faithfully used public transport if
her own two legs would not carry her as far or as fast.

'That's what I said. So get a move on, please. It's
clocking up money every minute you delay.'

Obedient, unable to argue with so stern a task-
mistress, Cassie pulled on her ankle boots, her coat,
gathered up her keys and fell in behind Bridie to go
clattering back downstairs. 'I'll explain everything on
the way,' Mistress McKay said over her shoulder.

And Cassie, feeling confused, flustered, ill-prepared
for confrontation, had to wait to voice the questions
which one by one suggested themselves.

Just days ago, the *Monitor* building had felt, if not like
home, at any rate like a kind of home-from-home.
Those rather scruffy premises behind the flashy façade
had been reassuringly familiar and friendly-seeming.

Now, as Cassie stepped into the entrance lobby in
Bridie's wake, she felt as though she were on enemy
territory, felt threatened and afraid. Her heart pattered
in her chest and she looked to right and left, fearful of
recognising anyone—or of being recognised.

'You can walk in with your nose in the air,' Bridie
had told her on the way here. 'Your name has been
cleared, you've been completely and utterly vindicated.
It's those others who have cause to hang their heads in

shame.'

But shame had always seemed to Cassie to bathe the guilty and the innocent, indiscriminately, in its cold, cruel light.

She was quaking as she stepped into the Editor's outer office, and Barbara's warm, welcoming smile did little to put her at her ease. 'Ah, Cassie, so there you are! I've been trying to get hold of you but there was no answer from your flat. I'm so glad you're here.'

'I wasn't going to come,' Cassie said, 'but *she* didn't give me any . . .' Looking over her shoulder for Bridie she found her staunch ally had deserted her, melted away, leaving her on her own to beard the lion in his den.

Barbara dialled the number on the internal telephone. 'Anthony, Cassie Murray's here . . . All right, yes I will do.' Then, replacing the receiver in its cradle, 'Please go right in.'

Cassie's throat felt constricted so that it was almost painful to swallow. Her chest felt tight, her nostrils flared. But she composed herself as best she could and lifted her hand to push the door. Before she could do so, however, it flew open and Anthony stood aside to admit her, saying, 'Come in, come in, make yourself comfortable,' in his most gallant manner, as though the unpleasantness of three days ago had never happened.

With his arms held aloft, he executed a neat little two-step across the room, picked up a chair for her and spun it round as though it were his dancing partner. 'Please sit down, do. Would you like some coffee?'

'No, thank you,' she said, slightly disarmed in spite of herself, for the man's charm, when he turned it on, was almost irresistible.

He stationed himself behind his desk, made a praying gesture with his hands, and asked her, 'Well, what can I say?'

'I don't know,' she answered honestly. Words might be merely dressings to cover her wounds. They wouldn't necessarily make everything all right.

'I was deceived, I confess it.' Now he opened his

hands like the covers of a book, and for several seconds
seemed intent on reading the contents. Without looking
at her, he eventually proceeded. 'It emerges that Roth's
friend, his ... er, source, Claire Thompson, is also a
good friend of Olinda Kington.'

'I know that now,' said Cassie, since Bridie had
already explained it. And, thinking of it, wasn't it
obvious? Paul Roth and Olinda Kington had been close
at one time, had moved in the same circles: it was
natural enough that they should still have acquaintances
in common. And those acquaintances would trust them
equally with a confidence.

'Young Layton was reluctant to tell us at first how he
got on to the Jane Oldfield story.' The book was closed,
palm pressed against palm, finger measured against
finger. 'But he was adamant that you were not
involved. He said you'd had nothing to do with it.'

'But then,' remarked Cassie acidly, 'he would,
wouldn't he? If we'd been in cahoots, he would be
bound to deny it.'

'Well, we thought of that, I have to say.' Now he
raked his hair with splayed fingers, appearing suddenly,
endearingly boyish. 'But Roth was persuaded that
Layton was telling the truth when he admitted he had
the whisper from ... er, Miss Kington.'

'And what about the call to Jane Oldfield? The one I
was supposed to have made?' Cassie demanded,
wanting to hear again, from this man's own lips, what
she had already been told by Bridie.

'Well, we can't say for sure.' Anthony swivelled in his
executive chair to stare at the wall behind him, at the
Turner print. 'But we know that Olinda Kington offered
to set up an interview for Layton, provided he would on
no account divulge his source. He was to pretend he
was a freelance writer and ... um ... your name was
used as a kind of open sesame. Your name and that of
the *Monitor*.'

'I wonder how she knew he had got the job on the
Inquirer,' Cassie mused aloud.

'My dear, the world of newspapers is a very small and incestuous one.'

'I realise that.'

'Anyway, I must tell you,' Anthony said breezily, 'I'm delighted with the way things have turned out. I'm sorry—really most humbly sorry—that I misjudged you. But I hope we can put it all behind us, eh? Get back to normal as soon as possible. What d'you say?'

'I don't think,' Cassie told him in considered fashion, 'that there's the remotest possibility of it.'

He was clearly unprepared for this response. Cassie had read of people's jaws dropping, but she'd never actually seen it happen before. His mouth fell open like a trap.

'I'm sorry,' she told him when he failed to make a response, 'but it's not the sort of thing I can just shrug off. My integrity has been called into question. I was put on trial by a . . . a kind of kangaroo court. Tried and found guilty. And no one had enough respect to give me the benefit of the doubt. How can I—with the best will in the world, how *can* I—simply put that behind me?'

'But we need you,' Anthony protested. 'The paper needs you. Your section, *In Touch*. Your readers need you, and your staff. You're one of our most gifted writers, a brilliant copy editor, I don't want to lose you.'

'No,' said Cassie softly, 'but you already have.'

He swivelled in his chair once more, offering her a view of the back of his head, where his hair was thinning slightly. 'But this is too much,' he bewailed. 'I mean, to lose *both* of you!'

'Both?' asked Cassie, confused.

'First Roth and now you.'

'First . . .?'

'I arrived at the office this morning,' Anthony explained wearily, 'to find a queue of people waiting to see me. A very irate Bridie McKay to inform me that I was a . . . a "blethering clodpoll", I think the expression was.'

Cassie couldn't help it: she laughed out loud to think of Bridie hurling insults at the 'stupid wee man'.

'Yes, indeed,' Anthony, ruefully, shared the joke,

smiling to show that he did not think the jibe
misplaced. 'Then there was Peter Playfair to talk about
the correct disciplinary procedure. Saying the Union
would demand a full enquiry into your case.'

'That's nice,' said Cassie, gratified. It was good of Peter
to try to ensure that she was not too badly done by.

'And then in comes Roth to give his notice. To say
he's leaving the paper because of all this brouhaha.'

'Because of . . .?'

'Because of the way we'd gone on. Jumping to
conclusions. He insisted you be reinstated forthwith. He
would resign. He seemed to think, for some reason, that
you wouldn't be able to work together, that your position
would be untenable. I told him he was over-reacting, but
he was adamant. Look, here, see for yourself.'

Anthony waved a sheet of paper under Cassie's nose so
that she might at least glimpse the wording typed upon it,
the bold, rounded signature at the foot of the page.

'I suppose he felt, after what happened . . .' She had
been articulating her thoughts, but her voice trailed off
as she remembered that Anthony Holt would not be
aware of her relationship with Roth, the stormy passion
which they had shared, which had brought them
together so powerfully, and now, with equal power, had
blown them apart.

'He feels very bad about it—well we all do. He
believes his continued presence around the office would
be irksome to you. So he's stood down, made way for
you, made it possible for you to come back and resume
your job.'

'Oh dear!' sighed Cassie. There was something peculiarly noble about the gesture. And something quixotic.
And something impulsive. It was just typical of Paul!

'Forgive me.' Anthony dropped his voice as though
they might be overheard. 'It's none of my business, of
course, but I have the impression that you and he were
. . . you know, quite close. That something other than
mere professional pride has been at work here.'

'You could be right,' Cassie acknowledged, getting to

her feet. 'If you like I shall go and see him. Talk to him.
I don't want him to leave the *Monitor* on my account.
That can't be the answer to any of our problems.'

'Absolutely not,' Anthony agreed. And, as she made
for the door, he put into words what she'd been thinking,
the glorious realisation which had dawned within her,
quite eclipsing her despair. 'Greater love hath no man
than this, than that he lay down his job for a woman.'

The trees in this lovely garden square were bare and
skeletal, but come the spring, thought Cassie, they
would be a riot of pink blossom. She wanted to be here
to see those trees in springtime.

She mounted the stone steps where the last of the
snow still clung, to rap at the front door of one of the
tall white houses. 'Please God,' she offered up a silent
prayer, 'let him be in. I have to see him now, this
minute, rehearsed as I am, ready as I'll ever be, word
perfect, knowing precisely what it is I have to say.'

But nobody came to answer her summons and when
she grasped the heavy brass knocker again and
hammered it against the metal plate, it seemed to send
shivers down an empty hallway, into empty rooms.

'Oh, Paul, Paul, you can't be out!'

She was on the point of leaving, had actually started
her cautious descent of those treacherous, slippery
steps, when she heard a noise behind her, heard a voice
say 'Cassie?'—say it questioningly, as though it might
not be she but an impostor.

When she turned back in surprise, her foot slid on a
patch of ice and she found herself sitting on the freezing
stone.

'Cassie, be careful!' said Paul, belatedly, as people
will. 'Are you all right?' And he came hurriedly to help
her to her feet, to dust her down with a solicitous hand
and make sure she was unhurt. His touch, at that
moment, was as familiar as it was welcome. But then
both of them, as one, remembered all that stood
between them to make strangers of them, and

simultaneously they became stiff, awkward, embarrassed. Paul released his hold on her as though some
impropriety had been committed. 'Are you hurt?' he
asked in an impersonal tone.

'No, I'm quite all right,' she assured him in the way
you might a passer-by who had stopped, more out of
politeness than any real concern, to enquire if any
damage was done.

'Do come inside.'

He went ahead of her, down the stairs to the kitchen,
where so recently they had taken breakfast together,
basking in the warmth of their love. 'I'll make us some
coffee,' he told her. And, as she perched on a stool, he
set about doing just that, busying himself as though to
keep from looking at her, as though to find some
displacement activity for his hands.

His mood was new to her, for she had never seen him
so subdued. Such an absence of emotion in so
passionate a man was both unnatural and disquieting.
Her nerves were in uproar, like birds put to flight,
sensing some disaster, an earthquake, long before the
first tremors shook their tree.

'I've just come from the office,' she told him,
clutching the side of the stool very tightly to steady
herself. 'Anthony told me you had resigned.'

The coffee-machine began to splutter. He went to the
cupboard for cups. 'All in all,' he informed her, with his
back towards her, his face averted, 'it seemed like the
best solution.'

'Best for whom?' she asked, and was surprised by the
plaintive note in her own voice.

'Well . . .' He turned to look at her consideringly.
'Best for you. Best for me too. Selfishly, we're the only
two who matter to me. The others can all go hang.'

'I do still matter to you then?' She seized upon this as
she got off the stool and crossed the floor to confront
him. 'I'm important to you even now? Please say if it's
the truth.'

'You damn well know it's the truth!' he flung at her.

And now, she thought, they were getting somewhere. Emotions were being stirred up, feelings expressed.

'There was never a moment when I didn't care. Not a moment when you weren't important, since I first set eyes on you.'

She looked at him standing there with the cups still in his hands. Looked at that long, lithe body, clad now rather carelessly in cord jeans, a checked shirt. She raised her eyes to gaze into his grey-green-blue ones, and wordlessly, telepathically, she made her response. 'And there has not been a moment, since we first met, when *I* didn't care about *you*.'

'Oh, Cass . . .' He all but sobbed the word, and he flung his arms wide, enfolding her in his embrace when she went to him, so that the china cups knocked against her back.

'I'm sorry,' he told her urgently, 'for everything. I should have known better. I was taken for a fool.'

'It's all right,' she assured him, and at last she knew for certain that it was, that she could forgive him—or, rather, that she had already done so, because she perceived that the rage, the bitterness, the vengefulness they had known, had all been engendered by love.

He slid his hands under her coat, eased it off her shoulders so that it fell about her feet. And he gazed with unashamed desire at that perfect figure, around which her slacks, her sweater, softly moulded themselves.

There was only one way, she knew, by which they might now, finally, be reconciled. And this time he would not have to sweep her up in his arms and seduce her, for the mutuality of their need was absolute, and all their actions, every caress, every endearment would flow from it.

He took her small hand in his much larger one, and went with her to the foot of the stairs, where they paused for an instant to exchange look for look, to make a silent pledge, one to the other. To promise that, henceforth, everything was going to be all right.

The bedroom was shadowy, the shutters half closed. The bed was unmade and rumpled as though he had spent a sleepless night. Paul seized the covers, the sheet, the quilt, and hauled them off, throwing them in an untidy heap, discarding them as unnecessary.

'Here,' he said, and when, acquiescent, she went to him, he eased off her sweater before ripping off his own shirt and holding her to him so that skin might touch skin and be flushed with a delicious warmth.

When, at long last, he kissed her, Cassie felt that she had been thirsting and might at last take a drink. Might take a deep draught of the love of which she'd been so cruelly deprived.

'I adore you,' Paul told her, 'you're more than anything to me.' And his mouth covered hers so that for a glorious few seconds they might have been of one breath, one being.

Imposing his full weight upon her he toppled her backwards on to the bed, his lips, all the while, loath to take their leave of hers. And he inserted a hand between the two of them to unfasten the waistband, the zip of her slacks, so that she might gradually wriggle out of them.

'Paul,' she felt duty bound to warn him, momentarily anxious, 'I ought to tell you, I don't . . . you know. I'm not taking the pill or anything.'

'Of course you're not. Why would you be? You were always armed against the opposite sex, no man was going to make love to you.'

'And then you breached my defences.'

'I did.'

'And you knew all along? Before, when we spent the night together? That I might get pregnant?'

'I didn't stop to think at the time,' he confessed, stroking a stray lock of hair off her face. 'I only knew I wanted you. My desire for you was everything. But afterwards it came to me. I realised that you might be . . .'

'Are you worried now? About if I should . . .?'

For a moment he loomed over her, peering down earnestly into her face, his blue-grey-green eyes dark with passion. 'Let's do it,' he said with new intensity, with greater ardour than ever before. 'Let's make a baby!'

And, as she responded with a smile, he dropped down on to her again, to make love to her with a ferocity born of pent-up longing and frustration.

'That is, of course,' Cassie mumbled, 'if we haven't already.'

'How was it?' asked Paul, greeting his wife as she walked through the door, wrapping his arms about her and treating her to a lingering kiss.

'Terrific,' she told him and, as he released her, she bent to unfasten the straps, to lift Alice out of her pram and to hold the squirmy bundle aloft. 'And how was your day?' For she still liked to hear news of the *Monitor*, of the activities of all her old friends and colleagues.

'Not bad. Interminable meeting with Ant. *Forward planning.*' He stressed the words, knowing how much they had always irked her when she worked on the paper. There was mischief in his eyes, and love, the two mixing together making him dangerously attractive to her. 'Then I gave myself the afternoon off. I wanted to be here when you got home, to hear how it all went.'

'How's Jenny getting on?' Cassie wanted to know, ignoring the question implicit in his words.

'Very well, I think. She seems quite capable, quite bright.'

Jenny Fieldhouse was the new star in the *Monitor* firmament. This year's winner of the Marguerite Palfrey Award, she had succeeded Cassie as editor of *In Touch*, and a highly competent job she was making of it, everyone said, though the pages lacked some of the spark, the flair which Miss Murray had brought to them.

'Anyway, never mind that,' Paul went on dismissively. 'Come along, tell me all about it.'

Cassie handed the baby over to its father, Alice, their beautiful daughter, whose tufty hair was tawny blonde, and whose eyes seemed by turns now blue, now grey, now hazel. And she went ahead of her husband up to the nursery, where Paul laid the infant baggage tenderly down. 'I'll get her changed first,' she said, 'then we can talk.'

'As you like.' He lounged there against the wall, taking pleasure in the sight of them, the two women in his life. 'Olinda was on the box earlier,' he said casually, conversationally. 'Interviewing the PM.'

'She's back from the States then?' asked Cassie with some surprise.

'So it would seem.'

After she had pulled her foul stroke, Olinda Kington had surprised everyone by announcing that she was going to America to work for a cable television company. Until the heat died down, Cassie had privately thought. Until the tongues stopped wagging. For the story of Olinda's efforts to discredit her had been fed to the satirical magazine, *Eye Spy*, and—while everyone took the gossip retailed in this publication with a pinch of salt—Miss Kington had not emerged with her reputation intact.

What had made her do it, Cassie had now and then wondered ever since. In retrospect it had been altogether foolhardy and, as an exercise in malice, almost certain to fail. But then, she would remind herself, hell hath no fury like a woman scorned.

Musing on it now, going over in her mind the events of one year ago, she went to the mirror to comb the velvety, dark hair, which swung free about her shoulders.

In a moment, Paul appeared behind her. 'Well?'

'Well, it's all agreed. Signed and sealed. They're going ahead and propose to publish in October. They seemed excited as I am.'

Cassandra Roth, novelist, grinned impishly out of the mirror.

Cassandra Roth, acclaimed young writer, former journalist, working mother—this was the *persona* she preferred, the one she lived and breathed.

Oh, and of course, she thought as he twined his arms about her, locking his fingers over her belly, and as she felt the play of his lips upon her cheek, Cassandra Roth, wife of the well-known Paul.

Harlequin Presents

Coming Next Month

Available in October wherever paperback books are sold, or through Harlequin Reader Service:

In the U.S.
901 Fuhrmann Blvd.
P.O. Box 1397
Buffalo, N.Y. 14240-1397

In Canada
P.O. Box 603
Fort Erie, Ontario
L2A 5X3

**A chilling new mystery by
Andrew Neiderman**

ILLUSION

They were madly in love.
But suddenly he disappeared without a trace.
Confused and disappointed, she began to ask
questions . . .

Only to discover that her lover had actually been dead for
five years.